THE SUN SETS IN SMYRNA: 1922

Book One in the Trilogy

Bess Georgakakos

Manor House

Library and Archives Canada
Cataloguing in Publication

Title: The sun sets in Smyrna : 1922 / Bess Georgakakos.
Names: Georgakakos, Bess, author.
Identifiers: Canadiana 20240511379 |
ISBN 9781998938186 (hardcover) |
ISBN 9781998938179 (softcover)
Subjects: LCGFT: Historical fiction. | LCGFT: Novels.
Classification: LCC PS8613.E5665 S86 2024 |
DDC C813/.6—dc23

Cover Art: Kelly Pasholk
Map of Smyrna: George Poulimenos
Cover design and interior layout: Michael Davie
Editor: Susan Crossman / Approx. 65,000 words.
Published in 2024 by Manor House Publishing Inc.
452 Cottingham Crescent, Ancaster, ON, L9G 3V6
905-648-4797 – All Rights Reserved.

Description: Was it absurd to believe so many cultures could coexist in a region where war has never ceased? In 1922, Smyrna was the beautiful cosmopolitan city by the Aegean Sea that was home to Turks, Greeks, Armenians, and Jews, to name a few. Taking place during the first genocide of the 20th century, *The Sun Sets in Smyrna 1922* begins with Vicki who finds her grandmother's short, but revealing, story leading up to the expulsion of Christians from the city of Smyrna in modern-day Turkey. This book - the first of three books - examines the journey of Celia, Vicki's grandmother, a teenaged Greek girl, who must overcome the horrors of humanity's malevolence toward one another, and her desire to maintain the ideology she was taught to believe. Separated from what is left of her family, and trying to outrun enemy soldiers and the inferno that has engulfed her entire beloved city, Celia tries to understand what the effects of rape, torture and evil do to an entire generation. As history has repeatedly exposed, the innocents are those who make the greatest sacrifice, and also reveal themselves to be true heroes… even when it's inconvenient to acknowledge them.

Funded by the Government of Canada | Canada

For all the refugees who have witnessed the abominable acts of humanity and their courage to overcome immeasurable losses. And, for KANE, the result of that perseverance and hope for the future.

Acknowledgements

I'd like to give special thanks to my editor, Susan Crossman of Crossman Communications, for her professionalism and for her encouragement in creating this publication.

As well, I am truly grateful to Manor House, and specifically Michael Davie, for giving me the opportunity to bring this publication to an audience.

Disclaimer

This is a work of fiction. Although it is based on a true historical event, the 1922 Burning of Smyrna—and woven through it are details from the author's own family history—a liberal use of imagination has forwarded the creation of this book. A great deal of research has gone into the writing of this book and most of the history is as accurate as the author could make it. But many of the names, characters, events, and incidents in this book are either the product of the author's imagination or based on real people, but fictionalized. It is not the author's intention to demonize any individuals or nations with this work but to demonstrate the hideous results of the failure of diplomacy and the heartbreaking impact of greed, anger, and cruelty ... and to demonstrate that despite generations of knowing the ravages of war, people are still capable of inflicting unspeakable horrors on their fellow human beings. Yet, growing out of the misery of conflict, can bloom the grace of hope and the flower of perseverance. Please note that some passages in this book may trigger feelings of anxiety in those who have experienced trauma in their lives.

About the Author

The only daughter of two Greek immigrants, Bess was born and raised in the east end of Toronto, where her culture had a vibrant presence. Stories of ancient heroes and a glorious history helped develop an interest in classical literature, the arts, and the human condition.

Marrying too young to study immediately after high school, Bess encouraged her four children to understand the value of a deep-rooted culture, family and community, while still exploring a world of constant change, self-awareness and independence.

She has lived in the Niagara Region for the past forty years, where, like many of us, she continues to strive for that magical balance of honouring a past and helping to shape the future.

Her first book, *The Sun Sets in Smyrna 1922*, is a testament to the struggles of those before us… ALL of those before us. Bess's objective is to acknowledge their journeys and their outcomes, and what it means for generations to come.

The attachments we have to our homes was what drove Bess to her other career in real estate. Our homes are extensions of our style, our security, our sanctuaries and our dreams. They are spaces where our souls find peace and it is in those moments of peace that Bess most enjoys writing.

*"**Bess Georgakakos** has written a captivating novel of love in the face of brutality, rape and oppression. Based on her grandmother's real life experiences during the 1922 burning of Smyrna, the author vividly thrusts us into the horrors of war... A teenaged Greek girl struggles to survive the fire engulfing her city as she searches for her family..."*
- **Michael B. Da**vie, author, ***The Late Man***

Preface

Most people's childhood memories are precious. No matter how large or how small a home is, we remember what was in our rooms and we remember the aromas that wafted in from the family kitchen. We remember the games we played in the streets with our friends and family members. We remember the trusted person we spoke to about our futures, and the teachers who taught us valuable lessons that were not found in a textbook. Even if we lived amongst hand grenades or in flea infested flats, there are moments, if ever so brief, when we will fondly remember the scenes, the smells, the stories, the sweets and the soothing sensation of a warm caress.

When children are uprooted—their homes overtaken by strangers, their family members killed or arrested and never seen again—something else happens. Hide and seek with Grandpa becomes a memory. Prayers are uttered in a refugee camp, if they're allowed at all. The girl everyone believed would grow up to be a dancer—because even at age five she moved like a gazelle—sits alone in an orphanage or a brothel. The idea of "happily ever after" disappears. Food, shelter and medical aid are the priorities, not basketball games or midterm exams. But when these children have a moment to think, a moment after the turmoil, even years later when they've settled in the foreign land that gave them refuge, they remember playing hide and seek with Grandpa, saying prayers in the grand mosque, and dancing in the courtyard where they felt they were the centre of the universe. The yearning for home, and the dreams it harboured, is immutable.

It's that yearning, that internal tempest, that rouses warriors into battle, a victorious one that they hope will soon lead them home.

Homer wrote *The Iliad*, somewhere around the eighth century BCE, and it is believed that his subject, the Trojan War, had taken place roughly four centuries earlier. The story, an epic ancient Greek poem, takes place in modern-day Turkey, close to what we now call Hisarlik. It recounts the ancient city's ten-year siege by the combined armies of the Greek city-states. It also introduces the world to the various heroes that western society has been familiar with for centuries. Over the ages, countless poems, stories, movies, and songs have been created using the same ancient characters, sometimes in entirely different narratives, and sometimes using only a hero's name or another defining attribute as a literary device. Achilles is the ultimate Greek warrior, Hektor the gallant protector of Troy, Odysseus the strategist and inventor of the Trojan Horse, and so it goes.

Some believe that the oral tradition of *The Iliad* began hundreds of years before Homer committed it to print, and that Homer was not a person but rather the representation of an idea. Because it wasn't written down until possibly the sixth century BCE, the epic had to be memorized. It would have been similar to the game where someone says they're going on a trip and begins by sharing with the group the one thing they're packing. The next person repeats what the first person said and then adds a different item to the make-believe suitcase. The third person does the same, and so on, until someone makes a mistake or can't remember an item. As the list gets longer, it's increasingly likely someone will forget a detail. This also brings to mind the game of Telephone where the first person whispers a short story into the ear of the person next to them, and that same story goes through the ears of everyone else who is playing. By the time the story gets to the last person it has usually changed, sometimes quite hysterically! And so perhaps it was for *The Iliad*.

There is always an expected benefit to war, at least for the winning party. Depending on the circumstances, the benefits can continue for ages to come. Of course, those benefits are material, in most cases: newly acquired land and its natural resources, access to trade routes, or slaves and concubines. At times, however, there is an intangible benefit, such as an enhanced public image, or even great glory.

Because a war involving the Greek people is at the heart of this book, a quick synopsis of *The Iliad* is in order. Leaders of Greek city-states have followed Agamemnon, the Greek leader of the army, to Troy in an effort to bring back Helen of Sparta, who has been abducted by Paris, the young Trojan prince. After a conflict with Agamemnon, the Greek hero, Achilles, ruler of the Myrmidons, refuses to fight. Achilles' mother, the demi-goddess Thetis, has previously told her son that his death will come shortly after Hektor's if he stays to fight in Troy, but that his name will have everlasting glory. He remains in his camp, bringing the war with Troy to a stalemate. Tired of an endless standstill, his loyal companion, Patroclus, dons Achilles' armour and, in disguise, fights the elder Trojan prince, Hektor. When Hektor defeats Patroclus, he removes his adversary's armour to keep as his own, as is customary, and in doing so, realizes he killed the young Patroclus, rather than Achilles.

Enraged, Achilles decides to honour the ancient code of ethics that requires him to avenge his friend's death by killing his murderer. But he has a problem: he has been left with no armour. Achilles sends his men back home to safety, but he chooses to stay. He summons his mother and asks her to bring him new armour. Thetis, in turn, appeals to the god of metallurgy, Hephaestus, who immediately goes to work and creates for Achilles not only a strong and durable shield, but an unparalleled work of art upon which he has embossed numerous intricate scenes. The shield depicts two cities, one engaged in battle, the other showing a wedding and even a scene from a court case. Homer also tells us of the sky, the stars, the sun, the moon, and the earth hammered into the shield. He describes a harvest, a wedding, a vineyard, and a bull being attacked by lions, while the herdsman and his dogs watch helplessly. And Hephaestus, the master of metal, frames the images with the ocean, edging it around the rim of the shield. The masterpiece includes all aspects of life: work and harvest, peace and war, children, workers, all the things that existed in the microcosm of a balanced Greek life. It was the life that Achilles chose to abandon for the glory of war and the achievement of his vengeance. While Achilles does defeat Hektor, as prophesied, he dies in Troy.

The Odyssey, Homer's other epic poem, is an account of what happened after the Trojan War. It focuses on Odysseus and his journey home to Ithaca. Looking for advice from his dead friend, Tiresias, Odysseus must travel to the Underworld. Once there, he sees Achilles, who asks him what he knows of his son and his home in Peleus. Achilles also tells Odysseus that he would have preferred to plough fields that he did not own than to lead the dead in Hades.

It wasn't until death that the mightiest and most glorious of the Greek warriors understood that home and the simplest life is the sweetest. But the thirst for glory overcame the hero. He learned his lesson too late for this lifetime.

What else have *The Iliad, The Odyssey,* and countless other epic sagas—whether recorded or orated—accomplished? They continue to encourage opposing sides to justify new conflict in the same lands. The politicians, victims, and heroes are different, their stories have changed, and displacement brings about a new home…eventually. But trauma is constant, and its effects reverberate through the blood of every generation thereafter… Lest we forget.

Table of Contents

Foreword

The Sun Sets in Smyrna takes place during a heartbreaking event in world history: the burning of Smyrna. Author Bess Georgakakos relates a remarkable fictional story based on her grandmother's true experiences just over a century ago in the aftermath of the gutting inhumanity of the First World War. Many thousands of people died during that brittle month of September 1922, and Thousands more escaped the carnage to forge new lives in Canada and elsewhere.

As I continued reading, the importance of the story Bess tells in this beautifully written book grew ever more relevant to our own world. Drawing on years of research and a powerful collection of family stories, Bess weaves an emotionally compelling tapestry of what it is to be human when the world around us is exploding into flames, both literally and figuratively. Of Greek heritage herself, Bess highlights the traumatic and bewildering exodus of Greek nationals from Smyrna—now Izmir—in what is now Turkey in the wake of the Turkish attack on almost anyone of non-Turkish background in 1922.

Over just a few weeks in September of that year, Greeks, Armenians, and people of countless other backgrounds, were savagely swept from their homes and communities—the men were abducted, the women were raped, and thousands of all genders were murdered. The seismic shock that blasted through the Greek community in the wake of the travesties committed in 1922 has reverberated down through the decades today in that one powerful question that the author asks through the writing of this book: how could this possibly happen to us?

I'm glad Bess brought this question into our lives in such impactful and unsettling ways, uncomfortable though it may seem.

As a person who has always worked with words, I share Bess's commitment to precision when it comes to the way we express ourselves, and the passion and compassion she brings to the story she tells in this pivotal book are a true source of inspiration. In the pages of this book, as in everything she does, Bess tells it like it is … with kindness and compassion and the type of sure-footed humility that is the powerful and empowering hallmark of truly great writing.

Some of our conversations during the course of Bess's work on this book have related to the shocking acts of horror that have been repeated over the course of human history. We have only to reprise Greek history itself to find stories of war that left innocent women raped and enslaved and dismembered men bleeding on the battlefield. War has been a constant in our world and it has existed whenever someone has wanted something someone else possessed. Particularly land.

In this book, Bess invites her readers to cross the bridges within themselves that are scary and uncertain—the ones that relate to power and powerlessness, vulnerability and resilience, fear and courage. With a graceful retelling of one young woman's determination to survive in the face of unspeakable and unfathomable danger she shows us how it's possible to put one doubtful foot in front of another and gradually build the resources of self-esteem and confidence that will fuel our passage to a stronger, more resilient, and more vocal sense of who we are and who we have it in us to be.

The fact that this novel tells the fictionalized story of Bess's own grandmother brings even more impact to the story, leaving readers with immense gratitude for their own safety in the here and now.

In this book, Bess focuses on the simple decisions that can impact an entire life: reach out and help someone. Take responsibility for your actions. Don't give up. For Celia, the main character of this epic story, success is about accepting her vulnerabilities and *choosing* her life. She invites us to appreciate any morsels of safety and security we can find. And, especially, she invites us to find the resources within ourselves to create our lives.

As you read this gripping story of a dangerous journey, Bess will help you simultaneously value peace on our planet while confirming the preciousness of each individual life upon it. She will encourage you to hold fast to your own dreams for your life and feel the siren call of the hero within you as we read about acts of everyday heroism that real people actually performed. And she will do it all through one of most gripping stories I have ever read.

This book truly is about the sun setting in Smyrna, but it also points to what happens after the sun sets: inevitably, and sometimes tragically, it also rises.

Bess has diligently created a powerful story that is guaranteed to ring through the years as a cautionary tale of what happens in a world where greed and hostility are allowed to percolate. She made the courageous decision to explore the topic through a book that tells a heartbreaking and valiant story that will no doubt bring readers to tears at least as often as it brings readers to their feet as they cheer for the journey the author takes her protagonist on.

Bess brings a calming confidence to the topic of an individual's personal evolution, and she does it with unflinching honesty and expansive wisdom. Read this book with a willingness to hear the voice of history and, more importantly, a willingness to examine how the story of just one individual can have a big impact on the generations that follow. And, who knows, maybe one day the story of the burning of Smyrna will seem to you, like it is to me, one of the agonizing examples of what happens when humanity leaves the playing field to the oppressor.

In peace,
Susan Crossman, author, *Shades of Teale*
Founder of The Awakening Author
www.awakeningauthor.com

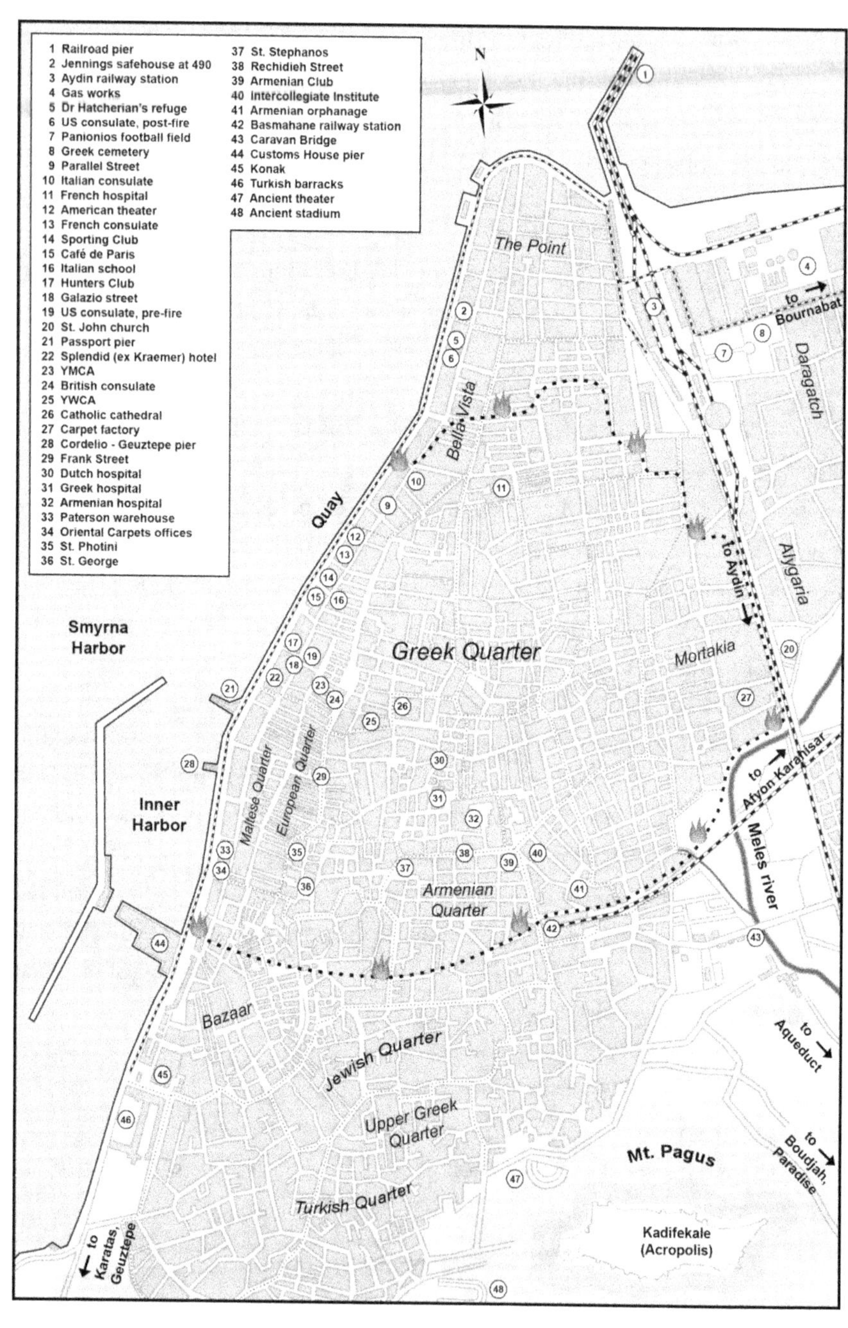

Map of Smyrna: George Poulimenos

Chapter 1

The Shield of Achilles

Vicki had cleared her bedroom closet and was almost finished emptying her dresser when she heard the side door open. There were only three steps up into the house from the side door, but her mother's footsteps were slow and heavy. *It's hotter than Hades and she probably went grocery shopping after work*, Vicki thought to herself.

Her mother, Nina, was only forty-two years old, and while the woman had been used to physical work from the age of five, even seated factory work wasn't easy, and Nina was exhausted after her half day of work. The constant back and forth movement over a sewing machine pushing a tiny needle through bathing suit fabric was tedious. Especially after twenty or so years.

Vicki heard the rustling of the grocery bags her mother had been carrying and their eventual plunk onto the tile floor. She dropped the tank top she was holding onto the dresser and went into the kitchen to help put the groceries away. The young woman knew it was a long bus ride from the nearest grocery store, and although the bus stop was only a block away, the temperature outside was a scorching 88 degrees, unusual for early June in Toronto.

"Hi Ma," said Vicki. Nina's English was limited, but since she and her husband only spoke Greek to their children, Vicki was fluent in that language.

Her mother nodded and, too tired to speak, plopped herself into the nearest chair.

"Oh, my lord, just kill me now. It's so unbearably hot outside!" Nina used her hand to fan herself. "I should have gone to get groceries with your father yesterday. What time did he leave for work?" she asked.

"About a half hour ago," Vicki replied, picking up the bags and placing them on the counter.

"What have you been up to?" asked Nina.

"Well, I'm packing most of my clothes into the suitcases," Vicki said. "I left what I'll need for the next few weeks. The rest of my stuff is in boxes, and I'll put them in the garage, for now. When Perry comes tonight, we'll load everything that will fit into his car."

"Okay," her mother replied. "Can you make me a coffee, my child?"

"Sure," replied Vicki.

"Oh wait! Don't bother. I just realized; your aunt will be here shortly to pick me up."

"Oh, I didn't know Thia[1] was coming," said Vicki.

"Yes, she's taking me to the seamstress for my final fitting," said Nina.

"Ah yes. I'm glad we told her the wedding was this weekend instead of three weeks away. We would have been cutting it close. By the way, Ma, where is my passport? I'll need it for the honeymoon. I remember checking it to make sure it will be valid. It expires in 1986, so it's good for another two years. I left it on the table, but did you put it back in the drawer in the dining room credenza?" asked Vicki.

"Yes, it's where I always keep them," said Nina.

The women heard a car honking and from the kitchen, Vicki saw her aunt's blue station wagon parked in the driveway. She went to the door and waved.

"It's Thia," said Vicki. "She's not getting out of the car."

"I know," said her mother. "The seamstress is expecting us in fifteen minutes." Nina gave a sigh and stood up.

"You're tired, Ma."

---

[1] Auntie

"I am," said Nina, smiling. "But what can I do?" She looked at her daughter and nodded. "Okay, I'll be back in about an hour."

Vicki smiled back and watched her mom walk to the car. She returned to the kitchen and put the groceries away.

Remembering her passport, Vicki headed for the credenza and opened the drawer that held the family's important papers. On the left side of it was a pile containing five passports, five social insurance cards, and five birth certificates. Vicki found her passport and picked it up. As usual, a fraying little notebook caught her attention from its place on the opposite side of the drawer.

It was falling apart and a few years ago, Nina had put it in a Ziploc bag to keep the pieces together. Vicki had always been curious about the book but had only once dared to pick it up. She was sixteen, when her father, Taso, had caught her flipping through the pages like it was a copy of the TV Guide. He barked at Vicki to put it back and never touch it again. He proceeded to yell at his wife for leaving it out in the open where "the kids could find it." That was when Nina had put it in the bag for safer keeping.

A few weeks after the incident, Vicki asked her mother what that had been about, and Nina said it was just something her father had found when he had returned to Greece to bury his mother.

"When I asked your father what it said, he replied that he couldn't bring himself to read it, knowing what she had been through." Vicki saw the look on her mother's face had a hint of confusion, but Nina concluded added, "I guess he just wanted to be very careful with it because it was so old and the pages so delicate. I think he just didn't want it to fall apart."

The book was small, maybe only nine inches long and seven inches wide, and was an azure colour except for a small white rectangle on the front cover where a name had been written. Vicki always assumed that the notebook belonged to her father. But this time, she took more time to look at it. She knew how to read, speak, and write in Greek and therefore understood the words: Βασιλια Αλεξιου (Σειλια) (Vasilia Alexiou {Celia}). Initially, she was confused. But soon enough, she remembered. It wasn't her father's name; it was her father's mother's name—and Vicki had been named after Yiayia (Grandma) Vasilia. It was only recently that Vicki had learned of her grandmother's maiden name. And she had never heard the name

"Celia." As far as she knew, everyone called her grandmother "Vasilia."

Although Vicki had met her, her grandmother had passed away five years earlier, in 1979. And now that Vicki would be getting married soon, she was feeling nostalgic, wishing her grandmother were still alive to share in the joy. She pulled the book out of the Ziploc bag and carefully fanned the pages. The young woman 1921). She realized it was a journal, her grandmother's journal. The handwriting was very neat and although some of the words had faded over the years, Vicki was able to read enough to understand.

Those years of Friday night Greek School are paying off, she thought to herself. As she flipped through the pages, Vicki noticed that the dates went as far as 1922. Vicki remembered that year was often mentioned in her family. She didn't know why, but she knew there had been a conflict between the Greeks and the Turks. She also knew that her paternal grandparents had come from Smyrna, a city that sits on the west coast of modern-day Turkey. Eventually, they settled in the Greek port city of Piraeus, where her father was born and raised.

Vicki's father and his own father, her papou[2] George, (" Γιώργη,") didn't get along very well. But her father adored his mother. He was the baby of the family, and clearly Yiayia's favourite. Like Taso, Vicki was not too fond of her paternal grandfather either. It was obvious that Papou favoured his own namesake, Vicki's younger brother, George. It may have been 1984 but old paradigms still reigned supreme, even in a modern city like Toronto.

Vicki took the notebook into the living room and hoped that with her decent Greek language skills, she would be able to understand what Celia had written. She did not have a formal education in Greek but it

---

[2] Grandpa

was the first language she had learned, and the only one she used to converse with her parents and their generation.

December 21, 1921

I finally decided to follow Kyria Antigone's advice and begin a journal. She had told me to do this two years ago when she was my teacher, but I thought it was silly. What would I write? What if someone finds this and reads my innermost thoughts and feelings? Especially Mama. Well, I finally found something to write about now.

I hate this. It's disgusting and not fair. I hate being a girl...no, A WOMAN, as they call me now. Not a girl. And NOW they tell me all about this?! Not BEFORE it happened. Now! And now I understand why some of the girls in my class are absent at times. No one told me anything until I saw it on my bloomers. Thank heavens I was home and not at school or church.

I quickly put on my nightgown and ran out of our bedroom. Poor Maria thought I was going crazy. She didn't see what I saw, of course, but she knew something was wrong. I burst into Anastasia's room. I told her what happened, and she told me to calm down, that it was normal, that I was a woman now. I froze at what she told me. What was normal about this?! My sister told me to wait in her room and that she would go get Mama. Afraid I was still bleeding, I sat on the edge of Anastasia's bed, and I cried like I have never cried before.

When Mama opened the door, I wanted to run into her arms. But when she and Tasia walked in and saw me crying, she didn't waste any time scolding me.

"Celia, stop behaving like a child! I got here just in time. Maria almost came in. You scared the poor thing. She doesn't understand what this is about, and you cannot tell her. You will frighten her. You're a woman now and she is still a child."

I didn't know what to say. I was speechless. I am bleeding from the most private part of my body and yet somehow Maria was her concern?! Anastasia remained in the room, quiet, while our mother hastily showed me what to do.

"This will last for three to five days. And it will happen every month."

"What?! No! I don't want this!" I was sure Mihali would have heard me if he had been in his room. Terror filled me, hearing that this will happen again and again. And if Mihali didn't hear my scream, he surely would have heard Mama slap my face and scream at me to shut up.

"STOP IT! Do you think you are the only woman who has experienced this? We ALL endure this every month, and believe me, you WANT to have this happen to you. If you don't, you will never have children and what man would marry you then? You should be happy you finally got it. You're almost fifteen and I was worried it was taking you so long. Maria is ten and I wondered if she may get it before you."

I glared at Mama, as my hand cooled the stinging on my face. I stopped crying instantly, as I usually do, when Mama screams at me. I didn't know what to say. "Thank you?" Or should I thank God for this? She was WAITING for this to happen and getting WORRIED? Didn't she think to tell ME what was going to happen to me? I was as much a nuisance to her as this ... this curse was to me. And I felt silly for not already knowing.

"I'm sure you will still have this by Sunday when we go to church. It's only two days away. You can stay home that day since you won't be able to venerate the icon." I listened to what Mama was saying but I couldn't understand any of it. Before I could ask more, she left the room.

Anastasia stared at me, and I could tell she pitied me. I didn't need her pity. I don't know what I needed but suddenly I felt like the beggar Mihali and I saw as we went to the Quay last week. I wanted to reach for something, anything, anyONE that would hold me and tell me that this wasn't my fault.

"Have you had any cramps the last few days?" she asked me. I shook my head as I wiped what was left of my tears. "It will be okay, Celia. You'll get used to it." My sister caressed my hair and looked up into my eyes, smiling with compassion.

I didn't want to get used to this. How I wished I was a boy! Mihali doesn't have to deal with this. And as I sit here, writing this while everyone else is in church, I have to wonder why God did this. Was this about Eve's sin? She DID disobey Him, and I've heard that we've all had to pay for that. But that was her sin, not mine. It's four days before Christmas, the birth of His Son. Everyone will be there, and my friends will wonder why I am not.

Maybe Mama is right. God always has a plan and as Baba says, it is not up to us to question Him. Only He knows and we need to trust and believe He will never forsake us.

Vicki read the notebook and smiled to herself. *Geez, I felt the exact same way Yiayia did. Only I knew it was coming. I had to ask my mother what they'd whisper about at times, mind you, but at least she told me.*

It felt a bit surreal to read about her grandmother and her sisters. She had only met Thia Anesta once, on her first trip to Greece in 1971; she had died a few years later. Thia Maria, the youngest of the family, still living, was now in her 70s.

Vicki had always felt a bond between herself and her grandmother because they shared the same name. But that was it. Her grandmother spoke little, and it didn't help that they lived on two different continents. Vicki had not had much time with her grandmother.

As the young woman looked up from the page, she realized that what she had just read had contained more emotion than she had ever experienced in her grandmother's company. Vicki had never heard the old woman complain, but she had never shown much joy, either. She flipped the page to the next entry and continued reading.

January 20, 1922

Again, with this nuisance! I shouldn't complain though. I was able to go to church yesterday before this all began. But a part of me also wishes I didn't go. It was heartbreaking to hear Father Dimitri tell us about the war in the East. He said that the Turks are losing but that some of our men have died. One of those men lived here in Smyrna, in the Greek Quarter. Father pointed out the man's wife, who was sobbing into her white handkerchief with one hand and holding one of her children close to her body with the other. I looked at them and started to cry. What if that had been us? I don't know how we would survive if anything happened to Baba. Mama would be so sad but, worse than that, she'd be even more miserable than she is now. It would be unbearable! Baba is usually able to calm her down and make her smile. But if he were gone...

I know Mihali would help since he has a job working with Baba. He's older now, seventeen in October, and he doesn't order me around as much anymore, or yell at me. I rather enjoy his company now that he's getting taller than me. He takes me with him when Mama asks him to go to the market if she needs something that is too heavy for her to carry. We also went to the Quay again this past week, even though it was bitterly cold. We sat inside the Café de Paris and overheard some people speaking English. They were from a place called Birmingham and we took turns telling each other what we thought they were saying. He's better at it than I am but even Mihali says I'm catching up to him. He says learning how to speak English has helped the Greek merchants of the city, while the Turks are falling behind. I don't care to be a merchant, but I do think it will help me be a better teacher. That's what I want to be. Maybe I can teach children to speak English. Greek children and even Turkish children. But my Turkish needs to improve if I am to do that.

I don't understand why there is always fighting between us and the Turks. Mihali said that they've been killing the Armenians in the north for years, and Greeks, too. They've been killing them in the villages, on the roads, anywhere they can find them. Those Turks! They enslaved us for four hundred years, but our side won the Great War. I don't really know what that war was about, but Father Dimitri said Mr. Venizelos, in Athens, negotiated so that Smyrna is now controlled by Greeks again. I'm not sure why it matters who is in control, because while the Turkish governor was in charge, we were still allowed to live here, just like the Turkish people are living here now that Mr. Sophopoulos is in charge. The Jews and the Maltese don't seem unhappy, either. Everyone keeps to their own people, but we don't hurt each other.

As we walked home from church, I asked Baba about the war in the East and when he thinks it will stop. He told me, 'only when people learn to live together in peace.' When Mama heard him, she said 'then expect it to never stop.' Then Mama told me I shouldn't concern myself with politics. I said I don't know what politics means, and she told me it's a good thing I don't know because that won't help me find a good husband. Baba said that priests shouldn't be concerned with politics either, and Mama gave him a sour look. He stared back at her, smiled, and shook his head.

"Celia, when we get home, I will put the chicken and potatoes in the oven. In about half an hour, go out and check on it, please. Tasia and I must deliver Kyria Aspasia's skirt. Set the table, so that when we return, we be ready to eat."

I just came back from checking the food and the potatoes still need to brown, like Mama showed me. They should be home soon. Why did she take Tasia with her to Kyria Aspasia's? I know that she's been teaching her how to sew for herself, but do they both need to take the skirt to the woman? She always does things with Anastasia. She teaches her to sew and cook. She caresses her hair all the time. I love Tasia's hair, too! It's nice and straight, easy to comb and doesn't have silly knots, or tiny hairs sticking out of her braids, like mine.

Once when Tasia was crying about something, Mama tried to console her and told that her eyes were too beautiful for tears. Why couldn't I have blue eyes, like Tasia and Mihali? Mama DID say that 'thankfully' Mihali and I were like her because we are tall and statuesque, while Anastasia and Maria take after Baba. I'd rather be short with blue eyes and straight blonde hair!

But I can't be jealous, though. Anastasia is never mean to me. She used to help me with my lessons all the time when I was younger and does the same with Maria, now. Tasia is always kind and helpful. That's why everyone likes her. Especially Mama.

Vicki read her grandmother's words and was grateful she didn't have a sister. She, too, at one time, envied the hair of some of her classmates. Her curly brown hair and brown eyes didn't seem to give her much confidence, but now that she was getting married, compliments came often. She was only nineteen but she knew Perry came from a good family and she had always known she wanted to be a mother.

It was the part about the conflict that made an impression on her, though. Vicki had heard about Smyrna—that it had once been ruled by the Greeks—and she knew much about history, both recent and ancient, from school and from other Greeks she knew. The Turks and Greeks had always considered each other enemies. While her aunt had told her the typical fairy tales most North American children hear, she had also taught her about the gods of Olympus, the myths and legends, and, especially, about Troy and all its glory. Vicki knew her paternal grandparents had roots in modern-day Turkey, but the coexistence of different ethnicities in Smyrna that Celia wrote about in her journal was fascinating to her and she wanted to read more.

April 23, 1922

Since the beginning of the month, up until this week, Holy Week, I've been in a daze. I finally told Julia about this monthly menace, and she told me she's had hers for almost a year. Not only that, but she told me where babies come from! I thought THIS was disgusting but to have a man do THAT to me? It's unthinkable. It's inconceivable. What was God's plan in making us this way? Julia's sister told her, though, that it isn't painful, and that it could even be pleasurable. How is that even possible? It was all I could worry about … until this week. Exciting news came to our family. Thank God.

Now I understand why Mama took Anastasia to Kyria Aspasia's! Yesterday was Easter Sunday, and this year, Mama and Baba wanted to celebrate Tasia's Name Day at our house, instead of Thio Anesto's like we've always done. They also invited Kyria Aspasia and her husband, along with their son, Antoni. Once everyone arrived, Baba announced that Antoni and Tasia were going to be married in June! They are perfect for each other. She is eighteen and he is twenty-one. I am so excited for them, both. Especially Tasia. She will make a beautiful bride. And he is tall and handsome, too. He held her hand all day and she beamed her smiles everywhere. Everyone was so very happy. I helped Mama as much as I could, and she, too, looked happy. She even spoke to me instead of yelling and asked my opinion on how to arrange the food on the table. She also told Maria to do as I tell her.

I can't wait for the wedding! It will be so much fun. Even Achilles' shield depicted a wedding. It's the happiest day of a person's life.

Chapter 2

A Generation of Dreams

June 4, 1922

The wedding was yesterday, and it was spectacular! Anastasia was gorgeous in the dress Mama made for her. She also made mine and Maria's. We all walked to the church, as the smell of the blossomed acacia trees escorted the beautiful bride all the way to the steps of Saint Photini. There was a last-minute change of the koubaro (best man), but everything else was splendid. Everyone was so happy, we danced until 2:00 am.

I saw a boy there who looked so very charming. I was dancing with my family and when the music changed to a zeimbekiko, the women went to sit. As I walked off the dance area, a young man walked past me, and I caught a glimpse of his emerald-green eyes. He smiled at me as he and his friends headed towards the band that had already begun its brooding tune. I turned around and stood still, watching him as he loosened his tie and lifted his hands parallel to his shoulders. His smile changed to a stoic pout, fitting for the song that lends to loss and heartache. My heart began to beat so that I could feel it throughout my entire body.

He began to snap his fingers to the rhythm of the music, and I could tell he was strong just by the way he moved. He was graceful but swift. I had heard one of his friends call him 'Ari.' I had so many butterflies in my stomach, my knees weakened, and I thought I would faint. I knew I must have been blushing because it became so very hot. I didn't follow Mama and the others to the table … I was so mesmerized by him, I didn't want to budge. When the song was finished, I looked around to find Anastasia, hoping she could tell me more about him, but she was sitting with Antoni. She had been looking at me, too, smiling, and I think she realized I liked Aris. I felt so foolish, knowing I could be so transparent. Did anyone else notice? Too embarrassed to broach the subject, I walked back to our table.

Kyrio Spiro[3] was there, too, and I spoke with him for a while. His daughter is in London, studying to become a doctor. When I told him I was going to be a teacher, he was impressed and very encouraging. I'm glad because Mama made me feel silly last week, when I told my parents that Kyria Antigone suggested I would make an excellent teacher. Baba agreed with Kyria Antigone and said I could start in September. He knew the man in charge of the teachers' school and would make all the arrangements. Mama scoffed at the idea.

"How is she going to find a husband if she is still going to school?' she asked. But Baba told her to stop being so agitated. 'It's only one year of schooling,' he said, 'and she will not have any problem finding a husband when she's done. Mama huffed and marched into the kitchen. Sometimes, Mama makes me feel bad for thinking the way I do.

Maria and I recounted the entire wedding day on our way home last night, laughing and giggling. We even talked most of the night when we got to our room. Poor Mihali could hear the laughter and came to bang on our door to shush us. Maria froze at first but then giggled and fell asleep shortly after. Through the shutters, I'm sure I saw the night sky changing colours on the approaching sun. I wondered if Aris was still awake. That was the last thing I remember before falling asleep.

When I woke up this morning, Maria was still sleeping. I went downstairs and expected to find Mama and Baba looking as happy as they did last night. But they were sitting in the courtyard, and Mama was wiping tears from her eyes. When I asked what was wrong, Baba said that the reason the best man was replaced yesterday was because hours before the wedding they found out that his father had been killed. Mama got up and said she had to go get ready for the funeral.

I asked Baba how he was killed, and he told me that the man was an officer in the army. He was killed in the East where the war was going on.

'Baba, I know the Greeks and Turks have always been enemies," I had to say. "Yet, I don't understand why we aren't at war here in Smyrna but elsewhere we are. Was this because of Troy?'

---

[3] In Greek, the vocative case of "Kyrio" is "Kyrie" (Mr.). For example, when referring to a gentleman named Spiro, he would be called "Kyrio Spiro" (Mr. Spiro), but when someone spoke to the man, they would call him, "Kyrie Spiro."

'No, Celia,' replied Baba. 'The Turks, or rather, Ottomans are not Trojans. In the 1200s and 1300s the Ottoman people moved into this area from the East. They took over much of the northern part of Africa and eastern part of Europe—including Greece—about five hundred years ago. Before that, we Greeks had lived here since before Homer. When the Ottomans took over, Greeks weren't allowed to go to church. They had to hide their icons, they weren't allowed to speak Greek, churches were burned. The Ottomans—or the Turks as they became known—wanted everyone to believe in Allah, the Muslim god. But priests and teachers continued to practise our ways in caves, in secret. Many of them died doing so. Finally, in 1821, as you've learned from school, Greece, with the help of other Christian nations, declared its independence from the Ottomans. The Ottomans were pushed back to, as we sometimes call it, Anatolia, or Asia Minor. Over the years, the Ottomans here in Smyrna considered Greeks and Armenians lower class, less than themselves. But through hard work and smart business minds, we flourished, often surpassing them. We became successful. And sometimes, jealousy gets in the way, and has made their hatred for us even worse.

'Then, in 1914 the Great War broke out in Europe. Germany caused it, so they were on one side. The British, French and Americans—who were also known as the Allies—were on the other. There were other smaller countries that supported them, as well, and Greece was one of them. The Ottomans, however, supported Germany. As the war raged, the Ottomans were pushed even further east. So, when Germany lost, as punishment for supporting the wrong side, the Ottomans had to give control of Smyrna back to the Greeks.

'The Ottomans are ruled by a monarch, the Sultan. But a man named Mustafa Kemal—and his soldiers—want the monarchy to end, and they want the Greeks and Armenians out of their lands.

'The problem is, however, that although the Allies support us because we're Christians, many are starting to prefer working with the Turks because they control the part of the country that borders with other countries that are rich in oil. And THAT is very important to everyone. Oil is needed for so many things now.'

Now, I understood what was going on outside Smyrna. I know that sometimes even my own aunts and uncles or friends' parents will call Turks and Jews horrible names but they don't hurt each other. I *asked Baba how it's possible for everyone to get along in Smyrna but not out in the countryside. He asked me if I knew why we aren't allowed to go on our own to the Turkish or Jewish Quarters. We do go sometimes to visit the Turkish family, the Sydins, but never alone. Kyrie Sydin and Baba knew each other as little boys, he had once told me.*

Before I could respond, Mama came down the steps of the house and yelled at him. She said, 'Simo, what are you telling her? Stop! The children don't need to know about politics! We all stay with our own, Celia. That's all you need to know. You were born a Greek, you will marry a Greek, you will die a Greek.'

She waited for me to leave before going to the funeral. I left Baba sitting at the table and didn't go back out to continue the conversation. As much as he seems to want to teach me some things, Mama wants to keep me ignorant of others.

A teacher? Vicki was astounded. She, too, had wanted to be a teacher. She was even accepted to all three universities of her choice. Last summer, before she met Perry, and just after her replies from the universities and community colleges, her father had come into her room to talk about her choice.

"So, what have you decided," Taso had asked.

"Well, Ba, I applied to the colleges in case I didn't get accepted to university but I really want to be a teacher. I know it's expensive and will take four years."

"What?! Four years? That's so long. What about college? How long will that take?"

"Two"

"Oh, that's much better. I think that's your answer."

Vicki didn't want to push the university option. She didn't have the money and knew that her parents would be taking on the burden of tuition. She nodded and smiled at her father, and he left the room.

Within the month, her parents and some family friends had arranged for Vicki to meet Perry, a nice Greek boy from a respected family. Unlike her grandmother, Vicki had decided to forego the idea of a career and do as her father suggested.

As she looked at the journal pages, Vicki felt saddened. She couldn't understand why, but she decided to continue reading.

July 9, 1922

Mihali and I went to the Quay again today. It's Saturday, so we thought there'd be plenty of English-speakers. We ran into the beggar again, and Mihali dropped a coin into the man's pan. When we got to the café, he made sure we sat where the sun wouldn't hit us. It was very hot but the server immediately brought us some ice-cold water and each of us ordered a pastry with cherries—they are in season. We sat between two groups of Americans. I overheard one man say he was from a place called Texas. His accent was much different from the accents of the people in the other group. My English is getting almost better than Mihali's, I think. I can't wait to start school in September.

I ran into Julia and her sister at the Quay, as well. She told me they were going to the theatre later in the evening. I told her about school in September, and she was excited for me. We promised to see each other sometime next week. The Quay was bustling!

The harbour was full of ships and there seemed to be even more tourists in the city this year than last year. As we finished our pastry a whiff of a nearby jasmine flower swept across the café. The plant grew between the café and the Sporting Club, next door. Even Mihali, who cares little of such things, smiled as he took in a big breath of it. It was a sweet smell that was welcome over the intermittent odour of the ships' fuel. Had we come earlier in the day, nothing could have overpowered the smell of bread and kadaifi.

It wasn't until Mihali and I got up to leave that I realized the people on the waterfront weren't all tourists. When I looked towards the south part of the Quay I realized a Greek ship, The Kilkis, *was docked, while hundreds of soldiers were lined up on the pier. Some were waiting to board the ship while others were waiting to get into the oncoming whaleboats. Once in those, they would take them into the harbour where other ships flying Greek flags were anchored. Even from half a kilometre away, I could tell the men were exhausted, their heads drooping. Many were bandaged or on crutches or leaning on a fellow soldier. Some were lying on stretchers.*

There were other crowds of people, not just soldiers, at the other end of the Quay, as well. Sailboats and row boats were lined up along the Quay, taking people with their suitcases and crates, while others sat in a section of the street. There seemed to be hundreds of people just sitting there, on the ground. Some had even brought donkeys and carts with them. Why were they sitting on the street?

'What are those people doing there?' I asked Mihali.

'They're probably Armenians,' he replied. 'Then again, the Ottomans have been attacking Greeks, too. They're probably waiting to get on board one of the ships.'

'Why are they attacking people?' I asked.

'Why? Because they're savages!' barked my brother. 'They want to rid the country of us and the Armenians. And if we don't leave on our own, they're going to force us … or kill us.' I felt like he had punched me in my stomach. I didn't know what else to say.

As we walked home, Mihali asked me if Mama had told me that our brother-in-law was leaving to join the fight. I was stunned. I told him I didn't know a thing, that she hadn't told me. I was upset with her for keeping it secret. Antoni had just become part of our family, and now he was going to fight? I don't know how Anastasia could bear that.

When we arrived home Mama was waiting for us in the salon.

'Where were you two!?' she shrieked at us.

'At the Quay!' replied Mihali with an equally authoritative tone. 'Baba said we could go.'

'No more. You are not to go to the Quay or anywhere else, again!' Mama shouted. 'Not now.'

'What?! Why?' shouted my brother.

'Because I am your mother, and I said so!' Mama screamed with a rage I had never seen.

'Mama, have you gone mad?!' asked Mihali, stunned at her fury. I couldn't control myself, either.

'You don't let us do anything! You don't let ME do anything, unless Mihali is with me.' I even surprised myself at my outburst. I think Mihali's words gave me courage to speak up to Mama.

'What did you say, Celia?' she asked, staring at me. I don't know if the shock of my insolence was what caused her to lower her voice, or the preparation for a greater eruption that we've all witnessed in Mama, before. I knew she was angry, but so was I. I didn't let her get to that eruption.

'I tell you I want to learn something, and you don't care. You don't care that I want to be a teacher, that I want to learn English. All you care about is marrying me off to a good husband. Am I that much of a burden to you, Mama?' I couldn't believe I said those words to her. I was shaking and Mama was seething.

'ENOUGH!'

We all recognized that voice. Baba burst into the room but before he could continue, Mama whipped her head and pointed her finger at him to be silent. He filled his cheeks with air and chose to let it out without a word. None of us wanted to say much more about it.

While Vicki recognized what the journal's events were leading up to and knew how surreal it was that her grandmother would write about it, it was the emotion, Celia's audacity, and hints of feminism in such a time that she found unfathomable and incredible. Even she, more than sixty years later, did not have such courage, Vicki thought to herself.

August 26, 1922

It was so hot today. I was supposed to meet Tasia today to go pick up her 'stefana' from church. I was shocked Mama even let me walk to her house alone. But we would stay in the Greek quarter, and I think that's why she let me go. I still wanted to ask Anesta about Aris. But she had forgotten about our plans, because when I got to her house, her mother-in-law said she had left. I looked for her on my way home, but I didn't see her until I arrived. She apologized, and said she was missing Antoni and not thinking clearly. Neither am I. It was so unbearably hot outside, I had to wash myself when I returned home. And my clothes. They smelled of sweat and something burning, like cigarettes or something. I hate that smell.

Mama had to comfort a sobbing Anesta. Since the day Mihali and I were banned from going to the Quay, Mama has barely spoken to me. As much as I envied the warmth she was giving my sister, I was glad Tasia had someone to comfort her, too. I could never be jealous of Tasia. She had seen some Greek soldiers walking through the city, beaten and bloodied. Why did they have to walk throughout the city? Why didn't they just go straight to the Quay along the waterfront? She wouldn't have to see them and be reminded of Antoni. They're almost as hateful as the Turks! They look dirty and smell horribly!

I hate this war. I'm afraid Father Dimitri was wrong. I don't think the Greeks are winning.

September 11, 1922

Mama and I went to the Turkish quarter for some of the spices we needed. She says their cinnamon and cardamom are better than ours. After that, we went to our market and bumped into Kyria Antigone. She wore her light brown hair in a braid, but it wasn't pulled into a bun like it usually is. I'm glad Maria had her as a teacher last year. And from what Maria says, she had the same speech for the first day of school: she smacked the pointer on the desk and told everyone to respect one another. I was so happy to see her, but Mama did all the talking with her, probably because she knows Kyria Antigone encourages me to be a teacher and wouldn't want me to bring it up. She towers over Kyria Antigone, and with that same stature, wants to control the conversation. I was surprised she even asked me to come to the market with her, but she probably just wanted help carrying the food home. I'm still angry at how she just wants me to get married and out of her way.

Mama and Kyria Antigone were very concerned. There were Turkish soldiers in the city now and they looked very mean. Kyria Antigone and Mama said that they had heard Kemal was in Smyrna now too, and things will change. I don't know how, but I heard them say that if 'war begins' we should all head for the Quay, for the ships to Greece.

'To go east would mean death, and I have heard many men are forced to walk until they drop dead. And to go north or south, would only mean more soldiers, anyway. Constantinople is chaotic too,' Kyria Antigone told Mama. Greece, or even the rest of Europe would be better than living with Muslims who were seeking revenge against the Greek soldiers, she said.

'We have to go by sea to get out of the city. I know people have already been gathering at the Quay for weeks, waiting to leave.'

I gasped and felt my stomach almost jump out of my body when Kyria Antigone said that. I wondered what people could have endured at the hands of our soldiers. Mama looked at me, puzzled, or maybe upset for interrupting their conversation. She turned back to the teacher and said 'Yes, God only knows. We should be going now.'

Mama didn't speak to me as we walked home. I didn't know if she was angry at me or worried about the war. I didn't know if I should say something. I don't even know if she would have wanted me to speak to her. She began to walk faster when we saw some Turkish soldiers along the way. Later, Baba said he had heard gunshots throughout the city, both yesterday and the day before, but Mama told him to stop scaring us. For the first time in months, maybe years, I saw Baba get very angry.

'Stop thinking that this will go away. These soldiers are different! And some aren't even soldiers. They're vengeful men from our own city. We should have already left, Angela!'

He yelled at Mama and told her that we must leave. He said he was going to call his uncle in Athens to see about getting a job there. Mama was silent. I don't want to leave.

That's where it ended. Vicki closed the notebook and put it back into the Ziploc bag. *My grandmother spoke English?* Vicki had never heard a word of English come out of either of her grandparents' mouths. She knew they spoke some Turkish, but that was it. And now she understood why Thia Anesta had never had any children. *I bet her husband never returned from the war.*

Vicki wished Celia had written more.

Chapter 3

The American Relief Committee

Stephen Herman witnessed the refugees flocking into Smyrna in late August of 1922, and as the American consul in the city, he knew of its history very well. Villagers had heard the Turkish nationalist army was approaching and they had gathered what belongings they could. Knowing how large and multicultural Smyrna was, they headed for its port. While they were accustomed to the constant appearance of different armies in their villages, the most recent—Kemal's army—was barbaric, and word spread quickly amongst the Christians that they must leave their homes and head west.

Many of these refugees went to the consulate looking for passage but only American citizens could be accommodated. Some of those who had married United States nationals had their paperwork rushed to get out of the city, especially if they looked like the local population. But there were very few people living in the countryside who were married to any foreigners, especially Americans. The rest decided to stay on the Quay until someone could provide them with answers to the question of where to go to find peace.

Herman was a tall man and relied on the use of a cane. He was a former reporter for the Boston Herald and enjoyed writing. Eventually, he was given a Foreign Service job in Berlin, and later, in Athens. Now in his sixties, Herman had been a consul for more than twenty-five years, eleven of those, in Smyrna. His sociable personality made him amiable to both Turks and Greeks, and he enjoyed the history of the region. Literature, golf, and archaeology were some of his pastimes in the city, and he had made some significant friendships, including one with Socrates Onassis, a tobacco exporter who was one of the richest Greek men in the city.

The consul had long been aware of the coming troubles from the east and knew that the Christian population of the region would soon be in trouble. But he could never have anticipated the magnitude of the chaos and devastation.

When Americans living in the city approached Herman and expressed concern about the scenes on the Quay and rumours of atrocities coming from the countryside, he had the same response for them

"It's my understanding that there will be a peaceful transition to Turkish governorship, and the new regime wants us here. As for your concerns about the refugees, I cannot help anyone who is not an American citizen," Herman would reply. "Our government has been very clear on its policy. We are not to intervene in the local politics." Herman was keeping his true thoughts to himself. He could feel a certain tension in the air. Those on the Quay were still primarily from the countryside, but there were many of them, and he didn't know where they were to go and who would be able to take them.

What he had heard about Kemal's army concerned him greatly and he hoped that it was only in the rural areas where men dared to commit such heinous acts—and not in front of the many eyes of cosmopolitan Smyrna. He also knew that the Greek Army was in shambles and nowhere to be found in the city any longer, leaving the Christians defenseless. Any Greek soldier that might be left in the city would be hiding and trying to find civilian clothing.

By the Labour Day weekend, Herman had sent two messages to Admiral Graham Boyd in Constantinople, updating him on developments and waiting for direction. The Chief Commander of the American presence in the region had heard of the migration of people and the retreat of the Greek Army and he knew that over the previous ten years, three million Christians had lost their lives at the hands of the Ottomans. The dead were primarily Armenian, although some had been Greeks and Assyrians. He was more inclined to ignore the conflict and allow the adversaries to work out their own problems. His job was to solidify ties with the Ottoman rulers or the nationalist Turks, whoever would control the trade routes and, more importantly, access to oil in the Middle East. Boyd was anti-Greek and anti-Armenian and had gone on record stating as much.

The nationalist Turks saw the benefit of maintaining control of the port city of Smyrna, as did the Sultan. Smyrna was prime real estate and the commerce within the city was extraordinary. So much so, that the Turkish and Jewish merchants resented their Greek and Armenian counterparts. Even the foreign businessmen sometimes preferred to deal with the less-savvy Turks to get a better price on products. But the Greek and Armenian populations had better access to products and had learned to leverage more efficiently. These Christians were also more entrepreneurial and open to new ideas and technologies coming from their western brethren, unlike the Turkish population which preferred to keep to their more traditional practices.

After failing to receive any direction from the Admiral, and having watched the crowd grow with each passing hour, Herman sent messages to prominent Americans in Smyrna asking them to meet at the American consulate, which was located just off the Quay on Galazio Street. It was evident to all that a crisis was unfolding and since lives and businesses were at risk, decisions needed to be made. Those present included missionaries, businessmen, medical staff, and representatives of major American companies. Group members quickly organized themselves for the purpose of remaining abreast of what was happening, and indirectly helping the refugees.

It was headed by Lyle Hirsch, a professor at the American International College who had lived in Smyrna since 1896. The American Relief Committee, as they called themselves, even designated a secretary and some of the members had been given specific tasks. Jonathan Lattimore, the recently arrived American missionary and work secretary of the YMCA, was asked to find food for the refugees. The committee also raised money for the refugees and pooled together their cars and trucks. They made certain that all vehicles and buildings would display some form of the American flag to avoid harassment by the Turks and the *chettes,* armed irregulars who looked for every opportunity to loot, assault, and even kill Greeks and Armenians.

When the *USS Lawrence* entered the port of Smyrna on September 9th, the Navy's Chief of Staff in Constantinople, Captain Charles Brice, was also on board. He had already seen what was happening along the 300-plus miles of coastline from Constantinople in the Sea of Marmara in the north part of the country, to the Smyrna harbour itself. Refugees from the countryside, and Greek soldiers fleeing from the battlefields, had made their way to any port where they could find passage out of the country and away from the approaching Turks.

Smyrna lay inland, behind a peninsula upon which the towns of Cesme and Yourla met the open Aegean. This peninsula sat just east of the Greek island of Chios and south of the island of Lesbos. As the ship entered the harbour from the west, the Quay lay directly in front of it.

Smyrna's natural shoreline went further east in the north end of the Quay, where The Point welcomed ships into Bournabat Bay even further east, behind the Railroad Pier. The railroad was the eastern boundary of Smyrna proper, and extended south towards Mount Pagos, just beyond the Turkish Quarters. North of the Turkish Quarter was the small Jewish Quarter, then the Armenian Quarter, and finally the Greek Quarter, which was closest to the Bella Vista area of the city, a more affluent area of Smyrna that lay right behind the northern part of the Quay. The Quay was the section of the city where its diversity was most evident. Jews, Turks, Greeks, and all others had businesses next to each other, some buildings being up to four storeys tall, some with awnings, some made of brick, some of wood, and others of stone.

The more prominent buildings on the waterfront were the Sporting Club, the Theatre of Smyrna, (commonly known as the American Theatre because its architect was an Armenian American), and—although the building was not on the waterfront,—the spectacular dome of the Italian School announced its presence on Parallel Street, just behind the Sporting Club. It echoed the Christian presence in the city. The Quay also had numerous hotels, including the German Grand Huck Hotel, which was next to the building of MacAndrews and Forbes, the licorice manufacturing company that had originated in Smyrna.

In the southern area of the Quay was the Inner Harbour, where most of the larger ships would lay anchor and where the Customs House Pier, Passport Pier, and Codelio-Geuztepe Pier were located. They jutted out into the harbour. Going east, or behind this area of the Quay, were first, the Maltese and then the European Quarters. They were beside the Greek and Armenian Quarters, but closer to the pier. The southern area of the Quay was also where many of the larger businesses, such as the carpet factories, were conveniently located for easy access to shipping.

It was the minaret of the Salepçioğlu Mosque that caught Captain Brice's attention. The beautiful place of Muslim worship had been built less than twenty years ago, in the Turkish Quarter. It was further south from the ship, but the tall, slender tower stood alone in that part of the city.

Brice found that while the city had looked magnificent from afar, the sight had become more disturbing as the ship dropped anchor in the Inner Harbour. There were people everywhere. In some sections of the Quay, the road allotment was more than fifty feet wide, but in others it measured only twenty-five feet from the buildings to the edge of the water. Packed in the narrower sections, people still managed to create a giant chain close to two miles long. Brice didn't quite understand what all those people were doing on the Quay.

There were many ships in the harbour but none were tethered to Smyrna. Brice expected as much, given his own orders. No government wanted to get involved with Kemal and the refugees his army had begun cornering onto the Quay. Allah was holding the chain by its tail and slowly swinging it like a serpent, taunting it and hoping it would quickly slither away once He let go.

While the American ship was ready to drop its anchor in the harbour in the west, the Turkish army had entered the city from the east.

Once anchored, Captain Brice, along with three of his men, boarded a whaleboat and went ashore. Brice ordered his men to wait on the pier and then headed for the American consulate where he would meet officials from the other ships and the American consul, Stephen Herman. He had no choice but to walk through the crowd that sat on the Quay and feel the stares of the filthy mass of people upon his immaculate white uniform. Even though Brice had served in the Spanish-American War and World War I, he had never witnessed such a mass of stagnant hunger, sickness, and despair. People's silent faces told him they had travelled for days from the countryside only to sit for even more days on the cobblestoned waterfront. Trying to understand the demographic he may have to deal with, he quickly scanned the mass of people for men. There were very few.

After arriving at the consulate, Brice was quickly updated on the city's status and was told about the newly created Relief Committee's plans, and how, if at all, the navy could help this organization. The captain informed the committee that while there were other American ships in Smyrna's harbour, the *USS Litchfield* would be the first ship to accept American evacuees. Many American civilians were packed and ready to leave as soon as the consulate could tell them which ship they were to board. The meeting ended with the knowledge that Kemal himself would be entering the city by the next day.

Chapter 4

History Repeats

Celia had already started stirring in her bed, but it was the sudden noise of a woman's scream that startled her awake. She looked over at her younger sister, Maria, who had just flipped the bedsheet off her little body and realized Maria had heard the scream, too.

Since there was only one other woman in the house, Celia knew it had to be their mother they had heard. Maria's eyes were already wide open and staring back at her older sister. The girls had their own beds, but they shared the room. The shutters weren't open yet, but the rising sun was poking light through the slats.

Was it really the scream that woke me? Celia wondered. There had been another noise, just before her mother's shriek, that had caused Celia to slowly stir. But it was the scream that had finally done it. The older sister put her finger up to her lips, signalling to Maria to be quiet.

My God, it's happening, Celia immediately thought to herself. Mihali said they were burning villages and killing people. *We're going to have to leave our home, like Baba said.* The young woman couldn't get her brother's words out of her head. *It can't be. I'm letting my imagination take control of my senses. This isn't happening in Smyrna.* Celia calmed herself but knew enough to remain guarded.

As she got out of bed and tiptoed to Maria, Celia replayed her brain's messages. *Yelling and a loud thud woke me up.* She grabbed Maria by the hand, and gently pulled her out of the bed. Neither girl uttered a word, as if they already knew something was wrong. After staring at each other for a few seconds, the older sister decided they would go downstairs to investigate the noises. Celia asked herself, *was this what everyone was worried about?*

Celia had become aware of her parents' recent anxiety. They never said anything to her directly, but over the last few weeks, she had heard them talking to each other, to neighbours, and to other family members. Celia was turning fifteen next Wednesday, exactly onc week away, and she felt her parents, particularly her mother, preferred to keep her from knowing what was happening in Smyrna.

Two days ago, she'd gone with her mother to the market, where they ran into Kyria[4] Antigone, Maria's fourth-grade teacher. The women spoke for a few minutes, and Celia noticed they were both anxious about "Kemal" and his troops advancing towards Smyrna. Kyria Antigone was in her late twenties, a shapely woman, and Celia's favourite teacher. She was always smiling and soft-spoken, but very direct, too. Her big brown eyes did much of the communicating with her students.

Smyrna was very cosmopolitan, with many foreign businesses flourishing in the Aegean port, and it even had a YMCA. In its current glory, in 1922, it was considered the most beautiful city in the world, the Pearl of the East. Although most students in her school were Greek, Kyria Antigone knew that conflict in this part of the world hadn't ceased since the rise of the first city of Troy, which was almost three hundred kilometres northwest of Smyrna. She knew that in a diverse city like Smyrna, life could go many different ways for children. But it would always depend on what they learned from adults. They were impressionable and easily molded by the stories they were told, the images they witnessed, and the realities they experienced.

The words Celia heard during the two women's conversation that day were the same as those she heard throughout the week:

"The Greeks have been turned back."

"They are burning people alive."

"They can't make every one of us leave Smyrna."

Little arguments would erupt when someone would dismiss the latest rumour and at times women would break into tears.

---

[4] Mrs.

"It's unfathomable that the Turks are advancing so quickly and with such fury. It's a lie," she would hear and become confused. There are Turkish people already living in the city. Why are they advancing with fury? Where to? But one question was in every conversation Celia overheard on the issue: "where would we go?" She never heard an answer.

When Anastasia, her eldest child, had come to see them the previous night, Angela had tried to calm her fears. Not having heard from her recently-wed husband since the day he had left to go to war, and listening to the rumours throughout the city, Anastasia feared she may already be a widow. Angela told her daughter God would keep them safe; as sure as the sun had always risen on their ancient city, God would keep them all safe.

But it was difficult for citizens to reassure each other and, more importantly, their children. It was now 1922, and more than 220,000 people were living in Smyrna: more than the population of the entire state of Delaware in that same year. More than half of the city's citizens were Greeks and Armenians and by the end of September that year, they would be either evacuated or dead.

Celia and Maria left their room and tiptoed to the top of the staircase. They both gasped at the sight of their father lying at the bottom of the stairs, bleeding from the left side of his head. The image pierced Celia's heart as tears filled her eyes. Simo moaned with pain, his arms moving slowly. Two men in uniform were standing over him, one holding a rifle, the other with a sword in his hand. She was no longer screaming, but Celia could hear Angela sobbing. She couldn't see her mother, but she knew it was her.

The man with the rifle noticed the terrified girls at the top of the stairs and yelled to them, motioning them to come down. Celia was incoherent and focused only on her father's body. She didn't notice the man's gesture. Both she and Maria became frozen in time, until they were startled by the soldier's louder second request which was accompanied by an abrupt strike of his rifle butt against the step. Celia, terrified, nodded her compliance and took the first step down. Maria followed her, holding her sister's hand with both of hers.

Celia could feel Maria's fear in her small hand, and could hear the little one sniffling. She had to tug on her sister to get her down the stairs. While she understood the apprehension, she didn't want to antagonize the soldier. As they descended the staircase, both noticed there was another man in the corner of the living room standing over their kneeling mother. Much of her hair was in her tear-soaked face and not in the usual ponytail she wore. That soldier, too, had a sword, but it was in its sheath.

That same man with the rifle motioned the weapon's butt towards the girls, telling them they were not to touch their father. Sobbing, they moved towards the living room, but Celia heard more voices coming from her parents' bedroom and the kitchen. The voices seemed to be more light-hearted, one even laughing. She could hear something breaking in the kitchen, things were falling to the ground. The girls were directed to go to their mother, who had stretched out her hands to her children.

Once passing the hallway where their father still lay, the girls ran to her, and Celia noticed blood coming from her mother's arm. When Celia's eyes widened and was about to ask her mother what was happening, Angela glared at her, whipped her head no more than an inch to the left, and pursed her lips, telling her to remain quiet. Celia said nothing and stopped the tears from forming, instinctively, as if she understood what the slightest noise could mean for her father. She wasn't quite sure how she knew this, but all the recent rumours in the city were suddenly running through her mind. The fears were materializing in front of her, only they were no longer just rumours.

"Stop lying, you dog!" said the man with the rifle. Greek wasn't his first language, but he could speak it well enough. He wore a red fez, and his brown uniform was dirty, with some traces of blood on one sleeve. He barked his demands and spit spewed from his plump lips, some of it landing on Simo's back and some catching in his thick moustache. Celia trembled as his inflamed dark eyes seemed ready to pop out of his head. She could tell the soldier was taller than her father and he was broader, too. Simo wasn't a very tall or imposing man. He was lean and only slightly taller than his wife, and Celia had equaled him in height. He also wasn't the sort of man who would physically challenge another. Simo's confidence stemmed from his words, his ability to converse. But the soldiers had no interest in listening to words.

"How many more are in the house? And how many more in the neighbourhood?"

"I'm telling you the truth, Afendi," moaned Simo, trying to put the weight of his body on his arms and lift himself up. But the Turk kicked him in his ribs, and Simo slumped back down to the ground.

"Baba!" shrieked Maria and jerked, almost leaping from her mother's arms. But Angela quickly pulled her youngest daughter's head into her own chest, keeping her from watching the scene.

Celia looked at her mother's face and could see a fear in Angela she had never witnessed before. The woman's mouth was quivering, while her eyes had become red and swollen from crying.

"You are not forty-seven! Do you think I am stupid?! Where is your son?!" yelled the soldier.

It was then that Celia noticed a very faint creaking above her and caught herself from looking up at the ceiling. Her brother, Mihali, was in his room on the second floor and must have been walking. She prayed that she was the only one who heard the noise and hoped he would stay up there, never to see what was happening. She also wanted him to be with them. He was only two years older than her but, right now, Celia knew he would try to protect them. She also knew there were too many for him and Simo to overpower.

"Why?" asked Simo, with confusion. "He is not even seventeen years old. You said eighteen!" Simo's eyes grew with horror, but a hint of defiance came from his voice.

The soldier walked over to Angela, grabbed her by her long, brown hair, and dragged her to the middle of the living room. Celia released her mother immediately but Maria held on.

"Mama!" the little girl shrieked, as she was dragged towards the stairs, with her mother. Before Simo could get up to help his family, again, he was kicked in the stomach.

Angela, expecting to be further assaulted, yanked her own arm away from her child so she would not remain with her, hoping to save Maria from any harm. The poor child had become crazed by what was happening, while a quick-thinking Celia crawled to grab her little sister and pulled her into her arms.

The women's screams and the soldiers' shouting created a deafening chaos in the room. All Simo could do was hold out his arm towards his wife and begin to weep as Angela did the same. None of his girls had ever seen Simo shed a tear. Never had they seen him beg for mercy, prostrate on the floor. As she looked at her father's face, Celia could see one eye begin to swell, while blood oozed from a cut just above it. Time suddenly froze and the young woman took a snapshot image of her parents, only a metre apart, and all the noises became muted in her head.

"Tell me where he is, or I will gut her like the sow that bore you!" yelled the intruder. He let his rifle fall to the floor and then pulled a knife from his side, putting it to Angela's throat.

Before the soldier could finish his sentence, everyone heard the trampling of feet, coming down the stairs. A voice called out "I am here! I am here."

Celia was relieved to see her brother and petrified at the same time. He was taller than Celia, just beginning to show signs of puberty. He had a few hairs starting to grow above his lip, and his shoulders were wider than they had been last September. Even his voice had begun to crack sometimes, which made all three of his sisters laugh. But because Celia, too, was in the throes of puberty, she was very careful not to embarrass her older brother too often.

As the young man came running down the stairs, he tried to kneel at his father's body, to help him. But the man with the sword instantly stopped him by pulling out his weapon from its sheath and striking Mihali with the handle. The precision and strength of the soldier's swing onto the young man's face caused Mihali's feet to whip into the air. He fell to the ground hard, his nose splattering blood on the wall as well as the steps of the staircase. Angela screamed at the sight of her son on the floor and tried to crawl to him, but her hair was being held tightly and she couldn't get past the room's entrance.

As if interrupting a horrible nightmare, two men came from the back of the house, carrying the rug from Celia's parents' bedroom. The men, who were not in uniform, but in plain clothes, paid little attention to what was going on in the hallway and living room. Nor did the family notice what the intruders were carrying. They were too concerned with each other's fate to turn their heads towards the looters.

A third man came empty-handed from the rear of the house, following the two thieves. Like the other soldiers, he wore a fez, but Celia noticed he had more adornments on his uniform. His black eyes were so large, and so piercing, very little white could be seen. His slithering motion emphasized his arrogance and pride. She gasped when he grabbed Mihali by his arm, and set him on his feet, only to slap him. Mihali tripped over his father on the ground and, again, fell on the stairs.

Fresh tears filled Celia's eyes, as she watched her brother roll over onto his side and curl into a fetal position. Her entire body wilted as she held onto Maria even tighter and began to sob into the little girl's shoulder.

"Get them both up and bring them outside. They are both of age. I will not listen to the lies of this infidel," said the commander in Greek. He spoke with no hint of an accent. Celia would have never guessed he was anything but Greek, had it not been for his uniform and fez.

Realizing her men were being arrested, Angela began to scream, freeing herself from her tormentor, who was left holding some of her hair in his hand. The soldier quickly put the knife back into his sheath and ran to get the mother. He grabbed her by her arm and slapped the woman hard across the face. All Angela could do was slump down on her elbows, sobbing and in pain. Celia did her best to keep Maria from turning around, as her own eyes scanned the room towards each member of her family.

The soldiers pulled Simo and Mihali to their feet and pushed them through the front door.

All three females continued to cry, Angela now bleeding from both her arm and cheek. Two more men came from the rear of the house, their hands full of household items and the jewellery box that had sat on Angela's dresser. Still, no one noticed the loot being carried away. The commander stared outside as his men were leaving with their captives and loot, and calmly turning his glance back into the home, announced, "you have one day to leave. When we return, you will not be here."

"Where are we to go?" asked Angela, who had just gotten to her feet while trying to dry her face from the blood and tears.

"I don't care," scoffed the man, still not taking the time to look at the woman. Instead, he jerked around to look at Celia. The man noticed the young woman for the first time. The sun was directly in front of the window, its rays beaming through the entire room. Celia's breasts were no longer those of a child's, and he could see their shape through her white cotton nightgown. She could feel him staring at her whole body, from top to bottom, and when his eyes met hers, she shut them tightly, shuddered, and turned away. The embarrassment and the terror fought each other to take ownership of her tears.

"You can choose to stay, but you will not want to watch," he said, as he snickered, glaring at the teenage girl. His expression horrified Angela, whose eyes doubled in size. With his head stretching for the ceiling, the sneering soldier sauntered out of the home.

As the door closed, mother and her two daughters ran to the window to see what was happening to the two men in their family. Celia saw her father, hunched over and holding his son close to him. But it was Mihali who was helping their father stand. The beating Simo had taken, told the young woman he would not be able to walk far, wherever they were being taken. She also saw other men from the neighbourhood lining up with Simo and Mihali. Kyrio Manoli was in front of her brother, his yellow shirt almost fully covered in blood. She could see he was bleeding from his right shoulder, where something had obviously pierced him. He, too, looked like he would not make it very far.

Angela and the girls were too afraid to go outside, but all three remained at the window. There were twenty or thirty armed soldiers in the street, some on horses. Even through the closed doors and windows, they could hear the soldiers berate the men, calling them names and telling them what fate awaited them in the east. Celia heard the many different soldiers speaking the city's three main languages: Greek, Armenian, and Turkish.

Within minutes, the prisoners were ordered to walk, but Kyrio Manoli couldn't move. He couldn't put weight on one of his feet. Celia looked down at them and noticed blood, totally covered his left heel. Many of the Greek men were shoeless, including Mihali. As the others walked past the injured neighbour, a cavalryman came up to him and yelled a question at him. Upon hearing his reply, the soldier took out his sword and drew it through Kyrio Manoli's chest, putting the man out of his growing misery. The screams Celia heard did not come from her house, alone.

Like Angela and the girls, Kyrio Manoli's wife was watching the death march begin, and saw her husband fall to the ground. Celia saw her run to her husband, her little girl, Alexia, following her close behind. The young woman put her hands to her mouth and held her breath as she listened to the little girl shrieking. The child tripped over herself trying to catch up to her mother, and Celia closed her tear-filled eyes.

"No more," said the mother. After watching little Alexia, Angela pulled her daughters from the image. She opened the window and reached for the shutters she had opened only an hour ago, just as she had done every other morning. But now, she wanted to keep the light and the horrors out of her home. Darkness quickly filled the room, and the mother stood motionless, not knowing what to do next. With her hands on her hips and her head looking down, Angela had to think quickly.

"Mama, why do they want us to leave our home? Where will we go?" asked Maria, still sniffling. "They took our things!"

"I don't know, my baby," replied Angela, with a breath of despair and anguish. She looked over at Celia, and her grief changed to panic. Her furrowed brows straightened, and her eyes widened, as if she had just realized she was not finished witnessing the horror of the apocalypse now taking place around her.

"Quick, go get dressed. Both of you!" she yelled. Horrified, Celia didn't understand what was about to happen, but she also knew that asking questions would only aggravate her mother. She grabbed Maria from the arm and walked quickly to the stairs.

The two sisters looked at the bloodstains their father and brother had left behind. The horror in the home's doorway only briefly kept them from running to get dressed, as their mother had ordered.

Within two minutes, the girls were back downstairs, looking around for Angela, who came out of the kitchen with bread and cheese. She had wrapped it in a cloth the soldiers had left behind. Her cheek had started to swell, but the bleeding had stopped.

"Have a few bites of each now. We'll put the rest away for later. Let's go," she told her daughters. The girls quickly nibbled on the cheese and took a bit of the bread, as they headed to the front door.

"Where are we going?" asked Celia.

"We are going to get Anastasia." Angela's attempt to sound calm didn't convince the older daughter. Celia could hear the faint quivering.

Chapter 5

The Battleground

Celia, only then, could put what she had just witnessed aside, to think of what could have happened, or could be happening, to her older sister. Anastasia lived with her in-laws, but Celia knew they were not in the home. Her sister's father-in-law had taken ill while in Athens, and his wife had gone to be with him.

The family's Turkish maid had been asked to stay the nights so Anastasia would not be alone. Angela had begged her daughter to stay with the family until her in-laws returned, especially with all the news coming from the east. Anastasia didn't want to leave her husband's home. Thankfully, she lived around the corner, and they could be with her in just a few minutes.

Immediately after stepping outside, they could hear little Alexia and her mother crying inside their home, as Kyrio Manoli's body lay still in the street. Women were coming outside, staring in the direction of the men's march and crying and holding their hands to their mouths in disbelief over what had just happened. One woman could be heard wailing from a few doors away. Celia looked around at her neighbours; none stayed outside very long. They didn't stay to console each other or hold each other. They all hurried back into their homes as if there was something to tend to.

Once outside their front gate and close to the dead man, Angela pulled Maria to the opposite side of her body and covered her eyes. Looking over her shoulder she called out to Celia, *"Min kitas,"* instructing her not to look, but the teen girl took a quick glance at their neighbour's body, making sure her mother didn't catch her disobedience. Kyrio Manoli's wife had draped her beige shawl over his face, but Celia could clearly see where the sword had entered his chest and ended his life. The blood was thickest near his heart.

Close behind her, Celia struggled to keep up with her mother, who was holding Maria by the hand. Angela walked very quickly; she was practically dragging the ten-year-old girl. The thought occurred to Celia to run up and offer to take Maria from her mother, to alleviate both of them. Before she could speak, Angela was looking behind her shoulder, and motioning Celia to hurry up.

The teenager could feel her mother's dread and panic trickle through the air between them. Celia prayed her sister would still be asleep, ignorant of what had happened in the neighbourhood. But she wondered what was going on in the rest of the city. Were the soldiers going to *all* the houses and taking the men? Everyone in the city was talking about the fate of the Greeks and Armenians, the ones who were most worried about the approaching army. Now, it was her sister she was most concerned about.

Without realizing it, Celia was already playing the different scenarios in her head, after witnessing what the soldiers could do. She purposely pushed all the other horrible thoughts out away and picked up her stride to keep up with her mother. She preferred to envision Anesta standing in her doorway waiting for them, beaming her usual smile.

Since she had been a little girl, Celia had always thought her older sister was much more beautiful than she was. Anastasia, who they sometimes called Anesta or Tasia, had long, straight, dirty-blonde hair and big blue eyes. Her delicate features and petite figure were the opposite of her younger sister's. Celia's hair was brown and curly, and she had brown eyes that, to Celia, were boring and plain. She thought having blue eyes and blonde hair was much better. Those lucky enough to have been born with both traits seemed so much more exotic, more enchanting, she thought.

From the moment the three left their house, the cries of women and small children could be heard from every household in the Greek Quarter. Some had gathered some of their belongings and were walking west, towards the Quay. As they walked, they could see some lone soldiers still coming out of homes, carrying household items. The uniforms of a few of them had traces of blood; some were ripped. Most of them didn't pay attention to the women on the street, and Angela was grateful for that. Besides, the women carried nothing of value to the soldiers. Nothing they couldn't get inside the homes they were looting. When the mother caught a soldier looking at Celia, she slowed down enough to grab her daughter and hurry her along.

As they turned the final corner, all three could see Tasia's house in the distance. Approaching it, Celia saw that the gate was wide open and twenty or so feet away, the front door was ajar. Celia heard her mother gasp as they passed the last house before Anastasia's. She inadvertently let go of Maria, who had slowed down enough to meet her sister, just behind her. Angela began running, her hand to her mouth, leaving the two girls about two strides behind. She was on a mission, and Celia saw a new strength, even anger, in her mother that worried the young woman, given all the soldiers in the vicinity. When she got to the gate, Angela froze, looking behind to see her daughters approaching. She raised her hands in front of her chest and stopped the girls from proceeding.

"Stay here with your sister," said Angela, looking straight into Celia's eyes.

Everything that had just happened in their home, the loss of her husband and son, the blood and tears she shed were nowhere reflected on her face. Anguish was absent, but fear lay ahead, and as Celia recognized it, she felt her stomach sink. The warrior she had seen for a few seconds, disappeared again. Slightly squinting, Angela's desperate eyes were asking Celia for understanding. She wasn't looking for a girl to understand her; she was looking for a woman to understand her.

The commander's glare jumped into Celia's mind, again. His posture, his antipathy, his smirk—all brought shivers to her skin. She now understood what her mother was fearing most.

Celia's friend Julia and some of their other girlfriends who had older sisters, had said how beautiful sex with a man can be, and how horrific, too. It was the talk of young girls who mixed facts with misinformation and the ickiness of biology. Celia hadn't spoken much with Anastasia about the topic, yet. She was too embarrassed, and the opportunity had never presented itself.

But there was no time to think about that, now. Celia tried to dismiss the soldier from her mind and tried to think happier thoughts about Julia and the other girls. Her friends were last May, and summer had brought the soldiers. She understood that what her mother feared was not beautiful … it was horrific. Celia couldn't let Angela go inside alone, but she also knew they couldn't take Maria inside the house either.

"Mama, you can't leave us out here. What if the soldiers come for us? I won't be able to fight them off and they will take us both! Let me go inside to get Anastasia. Please, Mama!" begged Celia.

Before Angela could voice her opposition to the idea, she looked at each of her daughters and sighed in resignation. She knew Celia was no longer a child, and probably understood her mother's fear. And she knew that Maria was still innocent. Every adult woman in Smyrna knew what war meant, especially if she was cursed with beauty

Angela thought quickly. She could not go inside, and risk losing two daughters in order to help one that might already be dead. Although she did not see the soldiers take any women or girls with them, Angela didn't want to take the risk. And she knew Celia would also be more tempting to a sinister soldier than Maria, or even herself. The house seemed too quiet for any soldiers to still be inside. It was best that Celia be the one to remain out of sight as much as possible, she finally thought.

She nodded her trust to Celia, and squeezed her daughter's hand, accepting she might witness the unspeakable inside the home. Angela's eyes swelled with tears again as her daughter walked past her, leaving the two on the road. Celia was apprehensive as she entered the courtyard. She slowly and quietly closed the warm gate behind her, smiling at her little sister.

Angela watched Celia walk away without realizing how hard she was squeezing Maria's hand. She could see that the door frame had been damaged and the door itself had a huge crack on it, near the handle. The mother also noticed that the house's shutters had not yet been opened, telling her that Anastasia had most likely been sleeping when the home had been invaded. Celia walked slowly up the two steps, and Angela lost sight of her as she continued into the dark house.

The young woman wanted to call out to her sister but she was too afraid it might scare her or, worse still, that a soldier might still be inside the home. She walked through the house, noticing some larger items were missing. Plates, candles, and glasses had been strewn across the floor. The curtains had been torn down, some of them were missing, as well. Chairs were overturned, tables moved, mirrors and glass broken. One of the windows in the kitchen had been broken and cutlery and old towels had been thrown in front of the hearth.

Celia had been in the house before and knew that the bedroom was close to the back. As she proceeded towards it, she passed a small room with a neatly made small bed. There was no sign of the Turkish maid.

She walked to the bedroom door but knew that if her sister was there, she wouldn't see her until she was standing in front of it. Feeling a bit shaky, Celia started to wonder if it might have been better to have stayed outside with Maria. *What if Anesta is hurt? What will I be able to do?* The door was slightly ajar, and as she came to it, she pushed it fully open. Celia breathed a sigh of relief when she saw Anastasia sitting on the edge of her bed, her back facing her.

"Anesta?" Celia whispered, but her sister didn't move. She didn't seem to notice Celia's presence and was staring outside the bedroom window which faced the stone wall of the neighbour's home.

As she came closer to Anastasia, she looked outside and noticed the fig tree that grew between the two homes bearing the last of its ripened fruit. Most of the items in the bedroom had been left untouched except for the bed and one of the pillows that had been ripped. Feathers were everywhere, some even in Anastasia's hair.

Celia slowly came up to her sister's bed, not yet being able to see her face. As she approached her, she noticed that her fingers were tightly interlaced, resting in her lap. She still wore her nightgown, but it was torn. There was nothing covering her thighs and Celia saw the bruises starting to develop close to her torso. She started to tremble as she noticed the blank look on her older sister's face. Celia felt numb, caught up in her own reaction of what she was witnessing, but she quickly caught herself.

"Anastasia," she repeated in a slightly louder voice. Anastasia continued to look out at the fig tree. As she sat next to her, Celia saw her sister's chest take a deep breath, her reddened eyes swell with tears and she let out a moan that was not loud, but so horribly disturbing. Her sister *had* heard Celia speak her name, but she could not utter a word in response.

Anastasia's body wilted to the floor, and she began to wail. Celia grabbed her by the waist and followed her to the ground. She experienced the pain of a loved one seeping through her skin, piercing her with fury, and she reacted in the only way she could: to hold her tightly, shed her own tears in unison and, after a few minutes, lift her back up onto the bed. After wiping her own and her sister's tears, Celia tried to speak again.

"Anesta, we have to leave," said Celia in a calm, soft voice. "They said they will be back and that we have to leave."

"I cannot leave. Antoni will come home, and I will not be here," replied her sister, half-crying and half-dazed.

Stunned at her sister's childlike tone, Celia took a few seconds to respond.

"Antoni will not want you to be here when the soldiers return," pleaded Celia and waited for her older sister to say something. She looked at Anastasia, whose eyes were finally dry. The silence was deafening to the younger woman; she didn't know what to do or say next.

Anastasia, still half-dazed, finally replied, but continued to look out the window.

"The night before he left, we made love." She picked at her torn nightgown and rubbed her thighs as she continued to speak. She closed her eyes and smiled.

"Then, I had a beautiful dream that I was a princess living in a beautiful city. I even wore a veil like the Muslim women do, and I had a diadem on my head. The city's walls were very tall, with twenty-two towers and the sun shone brightly above it. A young woman was there. She stood at the entrance, with her young son. I didn't know if they were leaving the city or new to it, until I asked her how long she had lived there. She replied '466 days, but it is time to go now.' That's all I remember of her. The sun was so bright. And then, I woke up." Anastasia's sapphire eyes finally looked at Celia and with agony and torment in her voice she continued.

"I didn't want him to leave. I begged him to say. He pointed to that fig tree outside our bedroom window and said, 'Tasia, I will be home by the time the fruit will be ready to be picked.' But he was not here."

Celia noticed her sister's voice had changed again, recognizing an anger she seldom heard from her lips.

"Four soldiers were here … but he was not," she said softly, again, changing her tone as if to excuse her husband for his absence. "It's as if Circe is keeping him from returning, as she did to Odysseus." Anastasia began to quietly weep again.

Simultaneously, the sisters shut their eyes as if that would stop the images from appearing. But closing their eyes couldn't keep an image from returning to Anastasia, nor another image from being created by Celia. Both were horrific.

Knowing they needed to act quickly, Celia hugged her sister, pushed her up from the bed, and gently motioned her to take a few steps. Anastasia continued to sob, and it was obvious from her walk that she was in some pain. She also knew that her younger sister could see her naked from the waist down. Celia kept staring at her sister's face. She told her to stand alone for a minute while she opened the wardrobe and found some clothes. She then turned back to Anastasia, making sure to look at her beautiful eyes, and asked her if she wanted help getting dressed. Anastasia stopped crying, gently took the clothes from her, and shook her head, giving her sister leave to exit the room for a few minutes.

Celia took the opportunity to run outside to tell her mother they would be coming out soon. She didn't wait to see her mother's relief, hearing the news that Anastasia was alive. When she ran back to the bedroom, her sister was dressed and waiting for her.

"Where are we going?" Anastasia asked.

"I don't know, yet. Mama and Maria are outside, waiting for us."

"But we need to find out soon," said Anastasia, in her simple tone. Celia didn't know how to respond, but she remained patient with her sister, guiding her to the front door. It was odd for the girls to experience this sort of exchange. Celia could still remember how Anastasia would care for her when they were younger, holding out her hand for her. But the roles had abruptly changed. Celia surpassed her sister in height and now strength and would need to guide her.

"Yes, we do need to find out soon," she replied.

"Yes, soon. Winter is coming."

They walked through the front door of the house and met their mother and little sister outside the gate. Angela immediately knew what had happened but said nothing to Anastasia. She only grabbed her and pulled her to her chest with relief. When the four were done hugging each other, they wiped their tears from their faces, turned to the road behind them, and began their journey.

Chapter 6

Returning Home

They had only walked as far as the house next door when Angela told them to stop. Celia noticed her mother take on the look of a strategist again. With her eyebrows furrowed, she stood perfectly straight. She looked directly at Anastasia. *What is she thinking?* Celia wondered.

"What is it, Mama?" asked Maria.

"Anastasia, was there anything hidden in the house that the soldiers may not have found?" she asked her.

"Like what?" replied Anastasia, still looking lost. She turned from her mother to Celia, who also did not understand what their mother was referring to.

"I don't know what you mean, Mama," said Anastasia, disoriented. Her inability to focus on what she was being asked frustrated her.

"Could your in-laws have hidden any money or gold or other jewellery somewhere in the house or in the yard? We all knew this might happen someday. Your father and I put some things away in a safe hiding place. They may have one, too," Angela said, trying to get Anastasia to focus.

Celia felt a small bite in her stomach for her sister. She couldn't understand why their mother seemed almost insensitive to what had just happened and was more concerned with buried treasures.

"If there is anything in the house, we may be able to use it," continued Angela. She was riled up, trying to plan for what was left of her family.

Use what? How? thought Celia. *We don't have any rifles or swords, and I don't think Anesta's in-laws would, either. Any jewellery or money will be stripped from us if we run into more soldiers.* The thought of soldiers scared Celia. She wanted to stay away from them as much as possible and not carry anything that would attract them to herself or her family.

"Not that I know of," said Anastasia. "They never told me of any hiding place. I know the soldiers ... they went into their bedroom and took some things that were in there, but I didn't see what they took." Celia noticed that just having to focus on her mother's question briefly brought her sister out of the fog, but only until she mentioned the soldiers. Anastasia's voice went quiet very quickly and she put her head down. Celia put her hand on her older sister's back, caressing it.

"No matter," said Angela, deflated, as she gently pulled Anastasia's hair back from her face. She softened her tone and said to the girls, "We need to go back to the house again. I need to see what we can take with us." She smiled and pulled Anastasia close to her, kissing her forehead.

Even though they were taken aback by their mother's sudden delicate tone and display of affection, the girls looked at each other and felt comforted by Angela's words. Celia was also relieved to see Angela taking a moment to be sensitive to Anesta's pain.

Angela was a noticeable force in the family, keeping it organized and running smoothly. And Celia's father was very content with their dynamics. Angela encouraged her children to be strong and confident. She wasn't the sort of woman who'd make grand gestures of affection towards her children or her husband, but they *all* knew they were her primary focus in life. She was demanding and had high expectations. Celia always found it more difficult to please Angela, than Simo.

However comforted, the three girls were still confused. *Where are we going?* they each wondered. They knew the soldiers had told them to leave, but they didn't quite understand where they were to go. The Quay or another part of the city? Another part of the country? Greece? And for how long? Will we return to our home in a week? Next year? Celia's mind was racing with questions, especially since she didn't know what was happening in the rest of the city. She couldn't bring herself to believe that this was what everyone had feared. She remembered Kyria Antigone had said people were already gathering at the Quay, but it seemed too difficult to accept that the time had come to leave Home.

As they walked back to their house, Celia found it disturbing how quiet the street had become. From inside the homes, through the open windows, she could still hear faint crying, doors slamming, even indecipherable whispering amongst families, mostly the voices of women. Very few were on the street.

Now, an ominous silence had overcome her family members' desire to speak. Celia stopped looking at the dirt and stared far ahead to the north, towards Mount Yamanlar. Intently fixing her eyes only on the blue sky and the mountain top, she could distinguish the footsteps of her mother and sisters. Her mother's were heavy and quick, Anastasia's were soft, barely noticeable, and little Maria's were brisk, trying to keep up with the adults, and stirring up most of the dust. The only other noise Celia could hear was Anesta's sniffling and her own heart beating and pulsating through her ears.

Once the women turned the same corner they had passed only a half-hour ago, they saw an older couple, their neighbours, coming out of their home. They were carrying a very small pot from the kitchen, a bag with what looked to be clothes or a blanket, and a small rolled-up rug. Celia looked at the items and thought to herself, *what could they possibly use a rug and a pot for?*

Kyria Amalia and Kyrio Spiro were in their mid-sixties. He was the first male civilian the women had seen since the soldiers had taken Celia's father and brother. He waited at the gate, slipping the tiny pot into the bag, while his wife went back inside the house.

It was a beautiful home, with many trees and flowers in its front courtyard. It was painted white with yellow trim and shutters. Celia and her sisters always wondered if the interior was as charming as the exterior. It was two storeys high but many of its upper windows were barely visible in the summer, as the copious branches of two chestnut trees surrounded the second-storey bedrooms, cradling them like a nest.

A third tree had been taken down last fall when the family's three adult sons were home visiting their parents. Kyrio Spiro had told them to stay a few extra days and chop down the dignified giant. As much as he loved the shade it provided, he was concerned the day would come when some of its thick branches would crash on top of the home or a passerby.

It took weeks to chop the wood, but the old man did it on his own, as his sons had left once the tree was felled. Because chestnut burns with many sparks, the cut wood was mostly used outside, primarily for the ovens. Kyrio Manoli had shared the wood with his neighbours, including Celia's family. He even offered some wood to his Turkish shoemaker and the Jewish rabbi who walked by when Simo was picking up his own share of wood. Kyrio Manoli knew all three of them.

The sun was already becoming bothersome. As the heat pierced through her light blue blouse, Celia could feel the dampness under her arms and across her temples. Her thick curly hair was held back by a ribbon that matched her blouse. Her mother made sure the girls had plenty of ribbons for their hair. But very often, Celia's would need constant retying since they would slide and release random chunks of curls.

She was glad to have stopped in front of the old couple's house, to catch her breath. Angela had been walking fast to get home, and all three of her daughters had to pick up the pace, especially Anastasia and Maria. Celia was now taller than her mother as well as her eldest sister, who was still preoccupied, and neglected to greet the old man. Kyrio Spiro was a lawyer, whose office was close to the Quay. He spoke English and French and had done well for himself.

The older couple had six children: three boys and three girls. One son, also a lawyer, was married and living in Paris with his wife, while their youngest son was studying in London, along with his older sister. Both of them were hoping to become doctors, something that was uncommon for a Greek woman. But, like Simo, Kyrio Spiro was an enlightened man who encouraged all of his children to educate themselves as much as they could. The other two girls were married, one living in Constantinople and the other in Salonika. Sava, their middle son, had chosen to stay in Smyrna, but was currently fighting in the Greek army, along with Anastasia's husband, Antoni.

Angela noticed the lost look on Anastasia's face. Normally, she would have made a discreet point of correcting her daughter's behaviour, but this time, she only felt the urge to cry when looking at Anesta. Instead, she decided to move her attention to the old man.

"Kyrio Spiro!" she said. She was so happy to see her neighbours, and yet, a bit envious that this man was still in the neighbourhood when she had seen so many others being taken.

Kyrio Spiro wore a black suit with a white shirt, unbuttoned only enough to see he was wearing an undershirt and to catch a glimpse of the man's collarbone under his wrinkled skin. He was slightly taller than Celia, but time had chipped away at his once robust physique. Celia remembered how Anesta had once described Kyrio Spiro as a man whose arms and chest could intimidate the mighty, or securely embrace and protect the weak. *She was right*, thought Celia.

He had always been nice to her and her family, a modest replacement for her grandfather, while he had been in America and, also, now that he had passed away. He may have been old, but in ways Celia could never understand, she knew Kyrio Spiro was not weak. His speech was always clear and powerful and at times he scared Celia and her siblings when he would yell at his children, particularly his sons. The boys were the neighbourhood pranksters, who more often than not chose to prey upon their sisters. Over the years, the old man angered less and smiled more.

The couple had been in Europe during the summer to see some of their children and had returned only three weeks ago. Celia hadn't seen them since Anastasia's wedding in June, when she had sat next to the old man for a few minutes and spoken with him about his upcoming visit with his children. In those few moments, she had come to admire him. He listened to her intently when she spoke about herself and her future and nodded with encouragement about her plans to become a teacher. His own daughter was studying abroad. They discussed the different people who come to the city speaking different languages; why did they come and what did they do? She didn't expect such attention and support from an adult, especially a man as old as Kyrio Spiro. He even told her she was a smart and beautiful young woman and that he would like to see her married to someone who was worthy of her.

"If you can keep practising your English, you will do fine as a teacher, and so many other things, my dear," said the old man, that night. "I encouraged my daughter to do the same and look where she is now. You know, she was a better student than her brother, even. They will make excellent doctors one day."

Celia remembered his words immediately upon seeing the old man in his courtyard. She was happy to see him, even in this time of chaos.

"Angela, I am glad you are safe," he called to her. "My wife and I are going to the Quay. There is a British ship in the harbour, as we speak. There are many ships, in fact. People are saying they may take us to Lesbos, or even Piraeus. Many of the American and British citizens have already left, so they must be willing to help us, now," he said with confidence. The tone in his voice quickly changed.

"I saw them take Mihali and Simo. I am so very sorry for you, Angela. It is a horrible thing to be grateful for being old," he said, nodding his head with his brows raised and eyes shut. He held his black hat in his hand, and as he opened the gate door, and came towards the women, he placed it on his snowy white head. He had lost very little of his hair over the years, and his moustache was just as white as his hair. Holding his arms out towards Angela, he shook her hand, clasping hers in between his two. His quick smile revealed his gold tooth, as he enthusiastically waved to Maria and nodded to the other two girls.

"Angela!" called out Kyria Amalia, from the doorway. "Get to the Quay as soon as possible."

Her tan-coloured crocheted purse hung from her wrist as she closed the door; she turned to lock it with the large metal key. She stopped, looking up at her home, as sorrow set on her face. New life and decades of joy had emerged from those stone walls. It occurred to her that to lock the door was absurd. The soldiers would not be stopped by a lock. But she locked it anyway. Celia wondered if the woman just wanted to do so, out of spite. She remembered how Kyria Amalia could be a bit short with the neighbourhood children. Often, she would hear the woman yelling at youngsters who would reach through her gate to pick the mulberries or peaches that had ripened on the bushes in her courtyard. Adults never dared to do so; she would berate them. The old woman pulled the key out of the lock and dropped it into her purse. Being that little bit more of a nuisance to the enemy just might give Kyria Amalia enough pleasure to get her through the trials she knew lay ahead of them.

As a fourteen-year-old girl, Celia couldn't possibly know what lay ahead. It wasn't in her nature to ask about "adult topics such as politics. And although she knew the Turks and the Greeks were always depicted as enemies in tales of the past, her parents always made certain that their children would treat others with respect, regardless of who they were and what god they believed in.

She remembered that her family and neighbours had rejoiced three years ago when they had seen the influx of soldiers into Smyrna. She didn't quite understand it then, but it began to make sense to her now. There was now a changing of the guard.

After locking the door, Kyria Amalia came up to her husband who took her by the hand and led her outside the gate. The woman's dull grey hair was neatly combed back and pulled up into a bun, as it had been every day since Celia had known her. Her crocheted cloche hat hid most of it, only emphasizing her sharp nose and noticeable overbite. As she came close to the rest of them, she looked at Anastasia and pursed her thin lips. Kyria Amalia's honey-coloured eyes teared up, but not enough to let any escape. She knew.

"May God be with you, my girl," she said to the young bride, trying not to make it seem obvious that she understood. She looked at all four of them and continued.

"With all of you." She quickly found something to say.

"You know, they took most of our jewellery and some other valuable items in the house, but thankfully, they didn't harm us. There were four of them. They killed Jason and Hecuba next door! Just slashed their throats in the courtyard!"

The old woman was loud, almost screaming, which wasn't out of the ordinary for her. But Celia became concerned, knowing there were still soldiers lingering in the nearby homes. She was glad to see the old man signalling his wife to quiet down, softly pumping his open hand towards her. Kyria Amalia checked herself and continued in a softer voice.

"Come with us, Angela. We'll all wait for the ships to take us."

"We cannot leave yet, Kyria Amalia," said Angela, not wanting to stay any longer. "We need to go back to our house. But we will look for you on the pier." Angela pulled Maria by the hand and started walking away, the other two girls following behind her.

"Do not be too long, Angela," called out, Kyrio Spiro. "I heard they have started burning some buildings in the Armenian Quarter, and the sooner we get on a ship, the sooner we can leave Smyrna. Our army and navy have left us behind and that bastard, Sophopoulos, is already on a beach in France!" The older man spoke with bitterness as he sharply waved his open hand towards the west.

"We will be there as soon as we can," called out Angela, not breaking her stride to get home. She turned and waved to the old couple, and then motioned her girls to hurry.

The words of Kyrio Spiro hit a nerve with Celia, even though she had heard of the possibility countless times over the last few weeks and that morning. *Leave Smyrna*, she thought to herself. *It's really happening. Leave Smyrna and go where?*

As she walked next to Anastasia, she felt her stomach sink. She was confused by Angela's actions. Her mother didn't consider where her father and brother were going, or if they'd ever see them again. She hadn't mentioned them to the girls since they had left their home. She hadn't even told Anastasia what had happened an hour ago, but her sister didn't think to ask, either. *What do you mean, 'leave Smyrna?' How?*

How will we know what is happening with Baba and Mihali and where we will reunite with them? And everyone else we know in the city? Our friends, aunts, uncles, cousins? Who will tell us where they are?

Celia had fallen behind her older sister, walking slowly, in her own daze.

The mounting voices of people in the streets had not yet reached her ears. Celia always had a plan, even though the life of a young girl was simple. She completed her chores, homework or any other tasks in advance, and quite aptly. Her books, drawers, and closet were all organized. And she always knew what tomorrow would bring. But now, she didn't have answers to the questions that kept piling up in her mind. Logic was not discernible at the moment, and she walked just as aimlessly as Anesta had done less than a half hour ago.

"Celia, ella!" called out Anastasia, startling her younger sister out of her state of bewilderment, and, suddenly, it was now Celia who was the one in need of direction. Celia quickly picked up her pace, catching up to her sister; she grabbed her delicate hand.

Chapter 7

The Dowry

Celia had reached for the same hand the day of Anastasia's wedding, three months earlier. She remembered how beautiful Anastasia had looked. She had stood in the doorway, watching in awe as the bride walked past the blossoming flowers in their courtyard. Through the courtyard trellis above, the sun had poked just enough sunlight to catch Anesta's beautiful blue eyes and reflect the joy within her. The daphne bush was in bloom, its tiny pink flowers sharing their sweet scent with its nearby guests. But it was the bride's smile that took everyone under her spell. As if in a trance, they would follow her to church like loyal subjects.

Angela had made the gown of white silk tulle. It had a bateau neckline with a sheath of delicate lace on the bodice. The skirt outlined Anastasia's slim hips, but was loose fitting and tea length, exposing her ankles. The sleeves were made from the same lace as the bodice, falling just below the bride's elbows. *She is a stunning bride*, Celia thought to herself, smiling and wondering if she herself would ever look as beautiful as her sister. Anastasia looked over her shoulder, beaming, and extended her hand to Celia, calling to her to hurry up.

"Celia, ella!" she had called out to her that day, as well, just as they began their jubilant walk to the church.

They were walking on the same road, Celia realized. *If only we could turn back time and go back to feeling that joy instead of this horror. Anesta wouldn't be suffering the pain she's enduring now and Baba and Mihali would still be here.*

It was at the wedding celebration that the young man, Aris, had caught Celia's eye, when he had appeared in the dance area. He, too, wore a white shirt that evening. Seeing Kyrio Spiro in his white shirt and Anastasia's extended hand reminded her of the wedding and made her wonder where Aris might be. If Mihali appeared old enough to be taken, she was certain Aris would have been, as well. Many of the boys she and her brother knew could have been taken prisoners, already.

Very often, Celia wished she had been born a boy. Especially since the winter, when her body had begun to change. Boys don't have to deal with this every month, she would tell herself. And when a baby was born into a family, it was evident how much more important boys were than girls. She heard the talk about carrying the family name, and the mere fact that boys were more capable of physical labour, and could therefore contribute more to the family.

The daunting hush in the street didn't keep Celia's mind from wandering. As they came closer to their home, she hoped that Kyrio Manoli's body had been removed, but wondered, if it had, who would have done so. His wife would need help to drag him and that, in itself, seemed so undignified, she thought. But who could lift him? He wasn't a large man, but it would take three women to get him inside his home. *And then what? Will he be buried today? Tomorrow? Will his wife stay behind to do it?*

She remembered his joy three years ago when his wife had given birth to Alexia. It was morning, in early summer, and the windows were open. Celia and Anastasia could hear the screaming from their bedroom. They had seen the young mother-to-be. But when the agony began, the two sisters looked at each other in horror, both dreading what womanhood meant for them in the future.

Later that evening, Kyrio Manoli was speaking through the gate with Angela, telling her that his wife was doing fine and that the midwife told him she would be able to have more children soon enough. He was so excited; the whole neighbourhood couldn't help but share his happiness that day.

No one was allowed to see the new mother nor the baby for forty days, according to tradition. But during that time, the only noise that could be heard through the windows was the newborn's cries and its parents' heartwarming chatter. Over the years, they all expected to hear of a new baby in that family, but it never came.

At times when the two sisters were alone, Anastasia and Celia often spoke of the screaming pouring through the windows that day. Yet, it was only recently while visiting her family that Anastasia told her mother and sisters that when Antoni returned from the war, she wanted to have a baby. Angela was elated, but Celia, who would be excited to become an aunt, was still trying to accept her own body's changes. And the sound of agony associated with the birth of the cute little girl next door still rang vividly in her ears. *And yet, we are the weaker*, Celia told herself.

It frustrated Celia when she'd hear about a man's rights to things, but she also knew she had to be respectful of her family's ideologies. They were the same as most of the city: men would have the last, sometimes, the *only* word. It would frustrate her even more when Mihali was part of the discussion. Her brother had no qualms about ordering his sisters around, especially when his parents weren't near. And Celia would comply most times. But as she grew older, she would question him when she disagreed with him, even argued with him. It infuriated her even more when he would try to make Anastasia obey him, even though she was almost three years older than him.

When Celia was ten years old, during one of their arguments, Mihali had told her there had been another son born into the family just before her. He died within days of his birth. The birth was so gruelling that their mother almost died, as well.

"She wanted to have another son so badly that she risked her life. But all she got was another girl. You! And to make matters worse, we ended up with one more. Maria!" he said angrily.

"Do you know what it will cost the family to get dowries for all three of you?!" he asked as he flung his hands up in the air. All Celia could do was stare at her brother. She was speechless, and, after a few seconds of silence, all her brother could do was stomp out of the room.

At the time, Celia didn't even know what a dowry was. When she found out, she was mortified to hear that a sum of money, or a piece of land, livestock, or some other form of payment had to be given to a suitor so he would agree to marry his future wife. A woman was a burden to her family, she realized. She often wondered how much her parents would have to pay a man when she would someday marry.

Walking next to her sister, Celia thought about that day for a few seconds. She remembered how confused she had been when her brother had yelled those words at her. But now, she wondered where her father and brother were, and in what condition. She and Mihali had become closer over the past year, and she worried about him now, especially remembering that he had to help their father stand as they marched away. Mihali stood taller than her father, who was bent over from the pain. *But how long could Mihali hold Baba? How strong is he?* Celia asked herself. The soldier's kick in her father's stomach flashed into the girl's head and caused her to flinch as she walked past the last place she had seen the two men in her family.

Chapter 8

The Tension Escalates

American missionary, Jonathan Lattimore, was compiling a small collection of safehouses in Smyrna. His latest was Number Three, and he was very happy about his new acquisition. He was determined to find shelters for the weak, the traumatized, and the orphans whose numbers were beginning to rise exponentially.

This latest was a small hotel, owned by one of the Levantine families in Bournabat, the wealthy suburb in northeast Smyrna. The Levantines were descendants of Europeans who had begun trading with the Ottoman Empire, decades earlier. Their name came from the French word "levere," or "to rise." When European traders, specifically the Italians and the French, came to the Eastern Mediterranean region—as far as Syria and Egypt—many married the Greek, Jewish, and Armenian people of the area. Thus, a new socio-economic class was created. These sharp traders and businessmen had amassed significant fortunes in Smyrna, and their lifestyles were a match for many European monarchs.

The hotel was a distraction, really, for one of the bachelor sons whose family had purchased it only a year earlier with a goal of curtailing his preoccupation with gambling. The property had a large lobby and ten rooms, and it was managed by an Armenian man and his wife. Now that the owner and his manager had bribed their way onto a ship in the harbour, Lattimore was able to secure the abandoned building, hoping to use it for the injured and sick old men of the city. Males between the ages of eighteen and forty-five had been taken prisoners, and those younger than that were with their mothers, lost, dead, or with someone willing to help them. It was the perfect location on Frank Street, which ran parallel to the Quay, and not far from his other safehouse at 490.

That's where Lattimore headed. He would inform Nurse DeBlanc of the new Frank Street house and ask her to take some of the few remaining supplies to the new location, before sending the men. Once he was finished organizing the transfer of people, he would look in on Mrs. Kontos and her young children, and then try to find someone who spoke Greek and English to accompany him to the bakeries to pick up some bread. It was only 9:00 a.m. and he was already short of breath from his walk back to the Quay. His slow pace allowed him to look at the faces of the people heading towards the waterfront, as well as the buildings along the way. Some, like the hotel he had just secured, had already been broken into and looted. Anything of value had been taken and all that was left were the beds, some linens, and a few pieces of furniture. That was all the little man needed to provide a haven for the men.

Before September of 1922, Smyrna had been a city with churches, synagogues, mosques, streets with English names, Armenian schools, French cafés, American tobacco companies, Jewish hospitals, and so much more diversity than Lattimore could have ever imagined. The cosmopolitan city bustled with trade and was one of the most prosperous cities in the Mediterranean, with a population of almost half a million. It was Islam's City of Tolerance, but the Turkish nationalists viewed it differently. While almost half of the city had Greek roots, spoke Greek to their children, negotiated primarily in Greek or French with merchants, gained new technologies from the United States or Germany, and prayed in Greek alongside Russians, Turks saw the city as *Giavour Izmir*, or Infidel Smyrna. Lattimore knew how blood-stained the region had been since the days of Homer's Iliad. He had heard about the more recent atrocities Muslims had committed against the Armenians in the northern part of the country, too. The co-existence of Christians and Muslims in Smyrna was not as utopian as he had imagined. He learned quickly.

When Jonathan Lattimore and his wife, Lilian, had entered Smyrna's harbour on August 2nd, 1922, the family of four had been awestruck by the many glistening marble buildings along the two-mile Quay. The sun had been just beginning its descent and the windows of the taller buildings captured its reflection. The Quay had a small trolley whose rails were less than fifteen feet from the water's edge, where dozens of fishing and sail boats were anchored. The larger ships would dock in the Inner Harbour, further south, where the Lattimores disembarked and passed through the Customs House Pier.

The entire world lay before the family as they stepped onto the Quay. Parisian fashion had found its way to Smyrna and women with hats and parasols strolled along the waterfront, while men with their summer boater hats sat in the nearby cafes. The American Theatre was presenting an Italian opera and many of the buildings had lowered their awnings to protect patrons from the blazing summer heat. For the Greek population, Athens, which was less than a degree south of their city, would often send the gift of a fresh breeze via the Aegean, reminding them the Motherland was not far, and finally free of the Ottomans.

Mr. and Mrs. Lattimore had two young sons who had already seen more parts of the world than most American children. Their parents emphasized responsibility and encouraged them to be tolerant of other cultures, while following the Christian values of American Protestantism.

Lilian was forty-one, three years younger than her husband. She was a soft-spoken, petite woman, thin and mousy, but with intriguing grey eyes that had hints of green in them. Her thin blonde hair had strands of grey but as she always wore it in a bun, it was never noticeable. Lilian suffered from constant anxiety and was sometimes prone to depression, but her husband's compassion and patience always seemed to calm her.

Jonathan, a Methodist missionary, was a short man, barely five feet tall and he had lost much of his blond hair. He had an awkward smile, as his mouth was disproportionately large for his small head. Originally from New York, he had contracted tuberculosi in his late twenties, which left him with a hump and a sluggish gait. He had moved his family into the Smyrna suburb of Paradise where many American families lived. It wasn't God's Paradise, of course, but it was as close as he had ever seen. Smyrna was mentioned as one of the seven churches in the Book of Revelations, and the religious connection touched Lattimore's heart.

He knew of the region's old wounds, but had also felt that the two primary ethnicities, as well as the Jewish, Levantine, Maltese and Armenian, co-existed fairly harmoniously in Smyrna, particularly since the arrival of the new Greek governor in 1919. He had heard from the American consul of Smyrna, Stephen Herman, that the city had not seen such prosperity and glory since ancient times.

Governor Dimitrios Sophopoulos had arrived three days after the Elite Greek Army had taken control of the city, an operation sanctioned by the Allies as reparations for the Ottoman Empire's support of Germany. The army had been met at the pier by the nationalistic Greek Archbishop of the city, and chaos had quickly erupted. Violence had broken out, as the new guard arrogantly vandalized Turkish businesses along the Quay, assaulting and humiliating the Turkish population.

On his arrival, Sophopoulos quickly restored order and severely punished those responsible for damages. His response came too late to placate the Muslims and, much to the anger of the Christians, the governor now had two enemies in the city: the Turks and the Greeks. But Sophopoulos would not be affected by historic rivalries. He had been sent to do a job, and he began doing it. He encouraged representatives of the other ethnicities in the city—specifically the Jews and Armenians—to have a voice in the city's affairs, he supported the creation of a new International College which was to open in September of 1922, and he discouraged the Greek Orthodox Church, primarily in the person of the nationalistic Archbishop, from meddling in the city's politics.

After the Great War and Smyrna's new governorship, the Greek army successfully began advancing east, trying to solidify their hold on an area many Greeks viewed as "once Greek." After five hundred years of Ottoman occupancy, many Hellenic soldiers felt they were liberating their people from the Sultan's long-standing chains. As they did, they subjected Turkish residents in outlying villages to ridicule, looting, and sometimes violence. And later, when Turkish forces regained control in the region, the treatment was reciprocated, often more brutally.

The Ottoman Empire retained control of the lands that make up modern-day Turkey, but it had its own internal strife. A nationalistic army was gaining momentum against the Imperial Sultan in Constantinople, hoping to create a republic. And although much of the country had Greek Orthodox Ottoman subjects, and much of Smyrna consisted of Greeks, the Greek army was seen as an invader and it eventually began facing defeat at the hands of the nationalist Turks, led by Mustafa Kemal.

By the time Jonathan and Lilian had moved into their Paradise home, Greek soldiers, who had been beaten, were steadily heading towards the Quay, retreating back to Greece. Now, on September 13th, it had been six weeks since Jonathan and his wife had arrived in Smyrna and two weeks since they'd seen the first refugees coming from the countryside, passing their home. The tension in the city had clearly escalated.

Chapter 9

Shields for Safety

From afar, Celia was relieved to see that Kyrio Manoli's body had been removed. Trying to ignore the man's blood on the street, Angela rushed to the front door, opened it, and ran to her bedroom. Her daughters stayed close behind her, not knowing what they were supposed to be doing. As they stood at the bedroom door, they saw their mother trying to push her brass bed. There was nothing on it except the sheets and mattress, and the rug that usually lay under the bed was gone.

She looked up at them, and they realized she was asking them for help. The two older girls ran to her, one next to her to push and the other across from her to pull. When the mother told them to stop, she kneeled and reached for an L-shaped piece of metal which Angela stuck into what looked like a knot in a floorboard, after which she pried the plank loose from its neighbours. None of the girls had ever known this hiding place existed. Most of the house was made of stone and tile. It now made sense to Celia who realized this was the only room on the main level whose floor was made of wood. Angela pulled out a cloth and opened it, showing the two girls what she was holding. She took a deep breath of angst but was relieved the soldiers hadn't discovered her hiding spot.

"It's not much, but we may need every little piece of value. They took what other money and jewellery we had this morning. Your father and I always made sure we had some jewellery of value out in the open so no one would think to look for a hiding place," said Angela.

As she unfolded the cloth, the girls saw four gold coins and a large gold pendant without a chain, which depicted the Argead Star. The four smaller gold coins were from the United States of America. Each of them had an Indian Head with a headdress on one side and an eagle on the other. They were all stamped "1907." Celia remembered stories about America from her paternal grandfather, who had returned from the New World in 1919, just after the First World War ended. His stories amused her, especially those about the "Indiani." He worked for the government and had spent time in the western United States learning about the indigenous people's history and their respect for the land.

Papou (Grandpa), once told Celia and Mihali that these people didn't believe in owning land, and that they moved from place to place. It all depended on the seasons, he explained to them. Papou Mihali died three months later.

"What are those, Mama?" asked Maria. She came to take a closer look at the items in the cloth.

"Your grandfather brought one gold coin for each of you," Angela told her daughters. "He could not be here when you were born, but he wanted to bring you what he felt he should have put in your cribs. I saved them in this handkerchief. It belonged to my mother. I had hoped to give them to your children one day and tell them about your grandfather." The mother stopped speaking for a few seconds.

"But that does not matter now. We may have to use them to get to Greece." Angela's voice cracked as she spoke.

"And this piece is from my grandmother," said Angela, holding up the pendant. "She wore it the day of her wedding. It was a gift from her husband's family. She didn't have any sons, so she gave it to my mother the day she was married. My mother gave it to me as I was the oldest girl in the family. My one brother became a monk and the other died at age eleven. When I told my mother how lucky I was to have it, she scolded me. She still let me have the pendant but told me it was shameful of me to feel lucky not to have either of my brothers carry the family name."

Celia looked at her mother and saw the sorrow on her face. Strands of her greying hair had fallen from her braid, and she pulled them behind her ear. Angela looked down at the floor, but quickly, with resolve and in a strong but broken voice said "We cannot waste any more time. There is no point in talking about the past. Maria, go to the kitchen and look in the cupboard where I keep all the thread and needles. Bring me the white spool and three needles." Maria obeyed and darted out of the room.

"Celia, go get the spring jacket I made you last summer, and get one for Anesta. If you can't find one, go into Mihali's room and get something she can wear. Quickly, each of you sew a coin into your hem and don't tell ANYONE about it unless you desperately have to. I should have done this before, but I couldn't in my worst nightmares, believe this was going to happen. I was silly not to be prepared. Your father was right," said Angela as she opened the armoire and pulled out a jacket for herself.

Celia looked at her mother with confusion, since it was already quite warm outside. But she quickly remembered it was almost fall, and no one knew where they would end up and when. It was still difficult to accept that she and her family were leaving their city.

Anastasia and Celia left to find their own jackets, and after they returned to the bedroom, they saw their mother sewing hers. As they came closer to her, they could see Angela holding one of the coins in place, as she sewed it into the hem of the jacket, close to the left side seam. When she finished, she ripped the hem on the right side, slid another coin into it, and began to sew it up, as well. As she did so, she told her two older daughters to do the same to theirs. She had taught the older girls how to sew, but Maria had only recently mastered threading the needle.

While the older girls each sewed a coin into their clothing, Angela went into the kitchen and rolled up the two mats that lay on the floor. She moved quickly and with purpose. She didn't want soldiers to come back and find them still in the home. She also knew that the sooner they got to the Quay, the sooner she'd be able to understand what was happening. The answers, if any, would be there ... at the Quay. Maria walked into the room and stared at her mother, bewildered.

"What are you doing, Mama?" she asked.

"We may need to sit on these, at the Quay, Maria," said Angela, trying to sound as if life were still normal. "I made these when I was a bit older than you. We used bits of old clothing, so we would not be wasteful,"

The older girls returned with their jackets, Anastasia holding the pendant. As the four of them stood in the kitchen, a sudden noise startled all of them. Each of their bodies flinched at the sound, but that was all their bodies could do. None of them moved. Celia looked at her mother and noticed she had her eyes pinned on Anastasia. As she slowly turned her head sideways to look at her sister, she didn't understand what her mother was staring at. But as she looked down, Celia noticed her sister's hands were shaking violently. She slowly grabbed them and intertwined Anastasia's fingers with her own. Maria's breathing increased enough to be heard, but still, no one moved or spoke for almost a minute. Angela finally made the decision to break the silence.

"I think it was just a piece of wood that fell." She quickly changed the subject.

"Did you finish the sewing?" she asked. "We'll be ready to leave in a few minutes. And don't forget your hats. The sun will be hot on the Quay." Celia ran out of the kitchen to get hers and Maria's from their room upstairs.

"Yes, we each put a coin in the hem. What do we do with this, Mama?" asked Anastasia, handing the pendant to Angela.

"I will keep it in my pocket. Just to have something quickly available," replied her mother, as she slipped it into her skirt. She opened the cupboards in the kitchen and found a small little pot just like Kyria Amalia's. She stuffed it and a small spoon into a bag. Celia returned with their hats, putting hers on and handing the rest to the others.

"Mama, what else shall we take?" asked Celia. "Shall we take the knife Papou brought back for Baba? The one he had on his bookshelf?"

The question startled Angela initially, but she quickly responded with a nod to her daughter. She had totally forgotten about it and didn't know if Celia's suggestion for bringing the Swiss Army knife would be for protection or the numerous other uses it could offer. But she was happy someone remembered it.

"Yes, I'll go get it from my bedroom," said Angela as she walked out of the room, looking distracted. She returned with a small linen bag tied with a drawstring. It seemed large for just the knife, but Angela handed it to her youngest daughter.

"Put it in that bag, Maria. And somewhere on the floor, I noticed two fallen pomegranates I brought from the market the day before yesterday. Maria, look for them and put them in the bag with the bread and cheese. If you see any other food we can use, put it in the bag, as well. I know we had some grapes, too, but I don't know if any are still there." The little girl, eager to help, fell to the ground, to look for the fruit. She found the pomegranates, and then opened the cupboard. Her eyes lit up, seeing the grapes. Maria grabbed them and ran the fruit to the bag.

Within minutes, the women were ready to leave. Angela threw the two tied-up mats over each of her shoulders, Anastasia held a canteen of water, and Celia carried the cloth bag with the food and knife. They walked past the blood by the stairs, and upon coming to the front door, they could smell smoke outside. *This is what Kyrio Spiro mentioned earlier*, thought Celia. The smell was faint, but something told her they didn't have time to waste. Regardless of how far the fire was, she knew that every other Greek and Armenian in the city was probably on their way to the Quay.

Outside the door, a parade of people was forming. Celia noticed that the only males in the crowd were young boys and old men. She turned to look how far the line of people stretched but could not see the end. She sighed and swallowed the little spit she had in her mouth. The unknown future was terrifying, but she remembered her father telling her that fear would always disappear once the decision was made to take a step towards it. "Just think of the dog you sometimes see on the street. It stares at you, hoping you will be scared. But once you move towards it, it runs away. Remain calm and logic will prevail."

The scene was heartbreaking. It was only 10:00 a.m., but everyone already looked wilted, their faces worn of traumatic events that had just unfolded and anxiety over what more was to come. Most were neighbours, a few were strangers, but Angela did not take the time to look for any familiar faces, and the girls obediently followed their mother to their front gate.

"If we go down the other streets, maybe we can get there faster," said the mother, as she looked at the groups of people walking by. Her apprehension was evident, but Celia worried it was her panic speaking ahead of logic.

"But, Mama, if we stay in a large group, wouldn't we be safer?" asked Celia nervously. She wasn't sure if her own fears were justified, but she glanced at her older sister to get some input. Angela looked at Anastasia, whose eyes were wide open, her lips slightly quivering, and then looked back at Celia. Her daughter was right.

She smiled at Celia, pride exuding from her weary face. Angela had a brief reminder of her own sisters, especially the one who lived in Smyrna. She wondered where Evanthia and her family could be, and if her husband had also been taken. There was no way of getting a message to her, but she would look for her on the Quay.

"You may be right, my child. We have to move, but we have to remain calm. Let's follow the others," said Angela, softly as she put her hand on Celia's cheek and held it there for a few moments. It struck her as odd, that she would take time during this chaos, this discord, to show any affection. It wasn't in her character. Her mother could be nurturing, but when Celia, and recently, Maria, had turned ten, Angela focused on teaching her daughters to be strong, efficient women and dutiful wives. She would comment on Anastasia's talent as a future seamstress. She laughed at Maria's childish humour and beamed at her new accomplishments at school or at home. And both Angela and Simo were quite impressed when Mihali began working with his father. Simo's coworkers had praised the young man, especially because of his fluency in English. Angela always beamed when Mihali walked into the room. Celia, however, couldn't remember a time when her mother displayed any pride in the daughter she herself had said, was most like her.

As much as Angela's hand on her cheek surprised Celia, the gesture seemed to invigorate her, as well. She noticed that her mother was looking at her differently. Celia was not sure if it was fear, or love, but the sides of her Angela's lips were slightly forming into a smile, and her cinnamon-coloured eyes were wide, almost tearing up. For the first time, Celia noticed the wrinkles that had formed close to those eyes and her mother's lips, feeling a warmth she hadn't experienced in a long time.

She couldn't remember her mother's last touch, or her face smiling back at her. Of course, she loved her mother, but Angela had little time for Celia, especially since Anesta's wedding. She was busy sewing, or cooking, or doing something else. She had no significant purpose other than this house, thought Celia. And she did not want to be like her. She wanted more. But now ... now, her mother was looking straight at her, and admiring her. *She does love me!* Smiling back, the young woman drew strength from her mother's gaze, took hold of the hand that caressed her cheek, and opened the gate for them to leave.

Chapter 10

Mothers and Their Daughters

The women hurried to join the group of walkers. Celia followed her mother's lead and didn't bother to address the familiar people she saw. Some were crying, others walking in pain. Many, particularly the young mothers, stood strong, trying to keep their children calm. Celia noticed the dazed look that Anastasia had worn just a half hour earlier on another young woman. A second woman had a swollen jaw, and she held it as she walked, holding her young son closely next to her. Everyone was carrying some portion of their lives with them ... a bag, an icon, a blanket, a picture.

Very few people spoke. And when they did, they whispered to one another. *Why?* Celia thought. But then she realized she, herself, was in no mood to talk, either. Who would listen to the horror she had just experienced? Everyone on the street had their own story to tell.

"Look," someone called out. Very few saw who spoke, but almost everyone somehow knew to turn and look behind. Just as Kyrio Spiro had said, there was dark grey smoke coming from the Armenian Quarter to the south. It wasn't very big, piling maybe five metres into the air, but it was a symbol of what could happen in other parts of the city. No, it wasn't very big, but it was certainly imposing, a stark contrast to the blue, cloudless sky.

Upon seeing the sight, the mob of people started hurrying, some pushing others. Almost annoyed by their reaction. *We already knew there were fires in that part of the city,* she mused. *Why are we rushing? We need to remain calm.*

As she was looking over her shoulder to see the dark smoke, she bumped into someone and caught herself from falling on top of the person, dropping the bag of food to her side as she stumbled. Her hat fell, too. When she turned around, she realized it was a young woman she had pushed to the ground. Anastasia bent over to pick up the bag, while Celia stood grief stricken and motionless over her victim.

"Voula!" shouted an older woman, as she bent down to help the fallen woman. The loud shriek startled Celia.

"Help me get her up!" the woman shouted to Celia. The older woman held on to her black flapper hat with one hand as she bent over to help the woman on the ground. Angela quickly came to Celia's defence. "It was an accident. My daughter didn't mean to hurt anyone."

By the time her mother had spoken to the older woman, Celia came to understand the stranger's concern. Voula, the young woman Celia had accidentally pushed to the ground, was pregnant. Very pregnant. As all three women helped to get her up, Voula winced and held her belly. She couldn't stand fully upright due to the pain.

"I am so sorry, I was looking at the fire behind us!" explained Celia, feeling horrible for the young mother-to-be. The teenage girl was almost in tears herself and, reaching out to Voula, realized she could do nothing to help her. Instead, she took her hands back again, bringing one to her mouth, in horror of what she had just done.

"What month is she in?" asked Angela, realizing the situation could get very tense very quickly.

"She has less than a month to go," said the older woman, as she put her arm around Voula's waist. "But she was already injured when one of them pushed her this morning. She hit her head on the wall and fell to the ground. They took her husband, my son. We've been walking for almost an hour already."

An older gentleman who witnessed the scene, came over to the women.

"There is an American man who has been helping the orphans and pregnant women in the city," said the man as he looked at Voula.

"He has taken charge of two of the bigger houses and turned them into clinics. I saw him stop a young Armenian woman yesterday, and after speaking with her, she went with him. I know her. I ran into her mother yesterday evening, and she told me that she went and saw her daughter in one of those homes. And she is being well-taken care of." The old man sounded very reassuring.

"He is a good man. He could have left this city already but has stayed behind to help people. You should try to find him. His name is Lattimore, and his clinic is at the Point, at 490, according to the woman. Dr. Mavridis' home."

The Point was at the north end of the city, and it was near the Quay, about two miles from where they stood.

The older woman motioned for her daughter-in-law to start walking forward. "Ela kori mou," she said softly to Voula.

"Can you come with us, sir?" she asked the older gentleman, with a louder, more pressing tone.

"I cannot," he said, shaking his head. "I am meeting my family at the Quay. I had to go back to the house for something."

Something, thought Celia. She knew he probably had a hiding place, too. Everyone in the city had been so afraid war would come to Smyrna. *They all must have hiding places*, she thought. She looked at Voula who was almost in tears and wondered if this young mother-to-be would be raising the child inside her, alone.

"Also," continued the old man, "I think you should go with someone who speaks some English. This American does not speak Greek or Armenian."

"I do not speak English, only a little French," the mother-in-law retorted. The woman sighed with exasperation.

"I speak a little," said Celia, offering to help in any way she could, especially since she had caused the fall.

"You do not!" scoffed Angela. "You only know a few words, Celia. You cannot help these women." The woman then turned to the two strangers, bowing respectfully. "I'm very sorry for your situation," she said to them, "but we cannot help you. I do apologize for my daughter pushing you," and she began to pull Celia by the arm.

"Mama, you and Baba told me how important it was for me to learn English. Especially Baba. And he was right. Mihali and I have learned to speak it well, now." Celia quickly turned her parents' encouragement to learn English into something she could now use, even to the dismay of her mother, who was shaking her head against the idea.

"I can come to find you on the Quay," said Celia, pulling her arm from her mother. "It's my fault they cannot continue without help. Don't you see how much pain she is in? I did that to her. I will take them there and come straight to the pier. I promise."

"You do not even know where you are going, Celia, and we need you with us. NOW!"

Angela stared at Celia and grabbed her arm again, trying to pull her away from the two women, hoping the discussion had ended. Celia knew that look on her mother. It was to tell her that Anastasia and Maria were more important than this young pregnant woman. As much as her parents differed from others who would malign foreigners, in particular the Turkish people, even Celia knew their own family and friends came before anyone else, especially strangers. But the teen became obstinate and furiously pulled her arm back.

"I did this to her! And you did this to all of us! If you had listened to Baba, we would be in Athens now! But you always want things your way." she yelled. She stood up straight and instinctively whipped her head in defiance, just as her mother had done earlier that morning. The gesture startled Angela into speechlessness, and she stood frozen.

"Celia! Stop!" called out Anastasia, shocked at her sister's audacity, glancing at her wounded mother.

The older woman took this opportunity to speak for her own cause, again.

"It would help us so much, if she speaks English," pleaded the mother-in-law. "We have nowhere else to turn. My name is Eleni Makroyiannis."

"Ok, Celia, I will not argue with you here." Angela's voice flattened with surrender, and she did not turn to acknowledge the old woman's introduction. She was angrier with her than she was with Celia.

"Help this young woman get to this safe place, but if you can, come back with that Lattimore man, or any other trustworthy man who will escort you. I do not want you walking the streets alone at the best of times. You cannot do so now! DO NOT WALK ALONE!" said Angela, raising her voice sternly, hoping she still held some authority over her daughter. While she understood their predicament, Angela hated that the older woman had used her daughter's compassionate nature to manipulate her and turn Celia against her. But she wasn't as impactful as Celia's hurtful but accurate words. They remained etched in Angela's mind, along with the faces of her husband and son.

"We will meet you in front of the French consulate," she said. "Look for the French flags. It's close to the north end of the Quay and you won't have to walk far. Do not go anywhere alone."

"I will not travel alone, Mama. And I will come as soon as I can," replied Celia, relieved that the argument was over and somewhat surprised it had ended so quickly. She felt ashamed for speaking to her mother as she had, especially after Anastasia had scolded her. But she knew her mother was strong, and Voula was weak.

"Are you sure you want to do this, Celia?" asked Anastasia, as she came closer to her sister. She looked at Celia with concern. "You do not have to go with these women. It is not your fault she is in pain. Stay with us, and we will go to the Quay together. Or they can come with us, and we can take them to this special house afterwards."

"She may not have that much time," Celia answered. "I will be fine, Anesta. We'll only be three streets over from the Quay, on Frank Street. You will get there a bit before me, that's all. You watch out for them and yourself, and I will help Voula. We can do this," said the younger sister, as she motioned to her family. Anastasia seemed more like her usual self and relented.

"Yes, we will," replied Anastasia, who stood straight as she spoke.

Celia felt like she had just found an equal again, only they were adult women now and not little girls. Between the two of them, they could support their mother, alleviate her anxiety.

Celia awkwardly hugged her mother, then her sisters. She turned to the young pregnant woman and Kyria Eleni, and put her hand on Voula's lower back, while the older woman held her opposite arm. Before beginning to walk, she looked to find the old man who had told them about Mr. Lattimore. He had been listening to the mother and daughter exchanging words but decided to get to his own task and had resumed walking.

"Where can we find this Mr. Lattimore? At the Point, you said?"

"If you go to the big old houses north of the American theatre by the Quay, you should be able to find him there! I hear he is sometimes seen driving in a black car, making himself available to those who need help. It will have an American flag on it."

Celia nodded her understanding of his directions, smiling with appreciation. She turned to the young pregnant mother and looked straight into her eyes with a sympathetic smile. As she took Voula's left arm, the pregnant woman smiled back and began walking.

"Thank you for your help, Celia. For me and my mother-in-law. I'm sorry to have taken you away from your family." Voula winced as she spoke, but tried to sound as positive as she could, humbling Celia.

"Thank you!" called out Celia to the old gentleman. But when she looked in his direction, he had already disappeared. A little embarrassed that she was shouting into the air, she turned and waved at what remained of her family. Her sisters waved back while Angela cautiously held up her index finger to remind her of the last words they exchanged.

Chapter 11

Don't Look Back

As Celia and Kyria Eleni held Voula, she could tell the young mother-to-be was struggling. Her breathing was mixed with sighs, winces, and moans as they walked the dirt road. It was hot and the older woman said they didn't think of bringing any water—or anything else—with them. Smyrna in September can still be rather hot. Even Celia was beginning to feel the thirst and realized that Anastasia had taken the bag she had carried, too. There was no water in it, Celia remembered, *but the grapes would be so tasty right now*, she thought to herself.

They passed many people who were also heading to the Quay, but of the two groups that admitted to having water, only one offered some to Voula and only Voula. All the two women had with them was a black purse that the older woman had wrapped around her wrist. It was quite large for a wristlet, and Celia could tell it was packed.

"When the Satans were finished looting our home, we were told we had to leave immediately, and Voula had already been crying." Kyria Eleni admitted she had not taken the time to plan for their journey after abandoning their house.

"If I had let her sit down, I was afraid I would not be able to get her back up. And after her fall, I was concerned the baby may come sooner than it is supposed to. She needs to see a doctor. I did not think to bring anything. Forgive me, kori mou (my child)." lamented Eleni, looking towards Voula.

"They killed our Armenian gardener right in front of our eyes. And the Turkish woman who works for us, was nowhere to be found this morning. She usually helps me prepare for travelling."

Celia didn't know what to say to the woman, trying to be respectful. She remained quiet and merely nodded.

"It is not your fault, Mama" said Voula, obviously short of breath. "Maybe we should just go back home, for a bit, just so I can rest and get some strength." Celia knew that going back was a bad idea. But she could see the pregnant woman straining to stand up straight, let alone walk. She also noticed a bump on the young woman's forehead.

"Voula, my child, we cannot go back." said Kyria Eleni. "I know how much pain you must be feeling, but we cannot. Returning home only repeats the sorrow. It begins all over again, and that is not good for you or the baby. We need to keep walking." Poor Voula nodded and leaned a bit onto Celia as she walked.

The three women continued north, but the people they passed were walking west, towards the Quay. The dirt road they were travelling had once been fifteen or twenty feet wide, with bright homes set back behind courtyards. But it had narrowed to become only ten or twelve feet wide, and it was flanked by older, darker, buildings whose doors opened directly onto the street. Some of the buildings were businesses; others were offices. Soldiers had already been in this part of the city, as evident from the personal items and papers strewn on the road. The women also came across some bodies, and because the streets were narrower, they found it difficult not to look.

Celia estimated that they were just behind the Café de Paris and that they should be at the safehouse area in the next half hour, given how slowly they had to walk. She also knew that the French hospital was close to the north end of the Quay and that it could be possible to get help there, especially since Kyria Eleni spoke some French.

As the three became acquainted, the smell of smoke continued to permeate the city. It wasn't just wood-burning smoke … it smelled of something else, but Celia couldn't identify what. Kyria Eleni and Celia tried to keep the conversation about the more pleasant past, about the teen's school and the older woman's family in Greece and France. But they slowly stopped speaking as dead bodies were becoming more and more frequent along their path.

The women approached a section in the road where seven or eight corpses were lying close to one another by a private school yard. They had no choice but to walk close to them. It wasn't the first time

Celia had seen a dead body, but those she had seen in the past had belonged to people who were about to be buried. Their bodies were clothed and handled with respect and love. Their eyes were closed, their hands folded on their chests. This was different. One body was of a man in his thirties or forties. His throat had been slashed from ear to ear and his eyes were still wide open. He had been stripped of his clothes, save his underwear. Celia's own eyes nearly popped out of her head and her nose shrivelled up when she saw his laceration. She heard herself gasp and immediately shut her eyes and turned away, embarrassed to have looked, embarrassed to have been heard by the other two women, and embarrassed for the man who lay dead. *No human being would have wanted to be exposed in such a way.*

As she walked, Celia asked herself many questions about humanity, but answers were impossible to find. *Where does someone find the indecency to do that to a person? The ability to hold them and draw that blade? And then leave them lying in the dirt, contorted like that?* As she looked to the opposite side of the street, she saw a stray ginger cat sniffing the body of a man; it ran off as soon as it saw the women approaching. Celia could see inner parts of the man's body lying across his abdomen. But it was the man's broken arm that shocked her the most. It looked almost normal, but it lay in the dirt in a most unnatural way. Celia became so nauseated, she could feel the convulsions in her stomach. And yet, her immediate reaction was to take a big step forward and slightly raise her left arm, to keep Voula from seeing what she had just witnessed herself.

Celia knew that Voula was older than her, and most likely closer in age to Anastasia. She even reminded her of her sister: her delicate features, her petite frame, her gentle mannerisms. But Voula, of course, was pregnant, and Celia felt responsible for her. Women had very little power in Greek society, but pregnant women were treated like rare porcelain dolls.

"Try to only look at the end of the street," said Kyria Eleni, firmly. "Do not shift your eyes from the end of the road, ahead," She spoke calmly, without any alarm or disgust at witnessing the bodies in the street and she tried to get the two young women to do the same. She continued walking with Voula holding her hand. The two young women couldn't help being distracted and shifting their glances.

Some of the dead men were shirtless, but all were barefoot. Their pants pockets were turned out, as well. One was robbed by a passing refugee, the women noticed. Two of the dead women were stabbed, one in the chest and one in the stomach. As the women walked past a third, they saw her torso was covered with a great deal of blood, it was difficult to see where her wound was, but the women, again, decided to look away. A few steps further, however, when Kyria Eleni saw the remnants of a breast just beyond the dead woman, she quickly and casually pointed to the building far in front of them, asking a random question to keep Celia and Voula from seeing the macabre scene.

As they continued, two cheerful soldiers came out of a beautiful home further ahead, their arms over each other's back. One soldier was wearing necklaces and bracelets he had found in the house. All five of them froze, upon seeing each other, the soldiers abruptly stopping their merriment. Celia felt her heart beating as if it had jumped outside her chest. Sweat seeped through her sleeves and glistened on her forehead. But she quickly gained control of herself, as if she had just been startled by the unexpected stray dog her father spoke of. She looked over at Kyria Eleni who gently nodded towards the road ahead.

"These ones won't bother us," she said softly to the others. The women lowered their heads and began to walk, carefully watching out of the corners of their eyes. As they passed the soldiers, the women could feel themselves trembling, Voula making a greater effort to walk faster. The men watched them walk past the house, and without saying a word to them, turned to walk in the opposite direction.

They approached the Bella Vista in the north end of the city, leaving the Greek Quarter to the south. Celia couldn't understand how some homes in this area had been broken into, or rather, targeted, while others were left untouched. She wondered if the brigade of soldiers had already come and left. There were no men, or anyone else for that matter, in the streets. Except for those heading in the Quay's direction, and those that lay dead, the street was deserted and the majority of buildings looked abandoned.

It was close to noon, and knowing the city quite well, Celia guessed they were a few streets behind the French Consulate and the American theatre. She and Mihali would often come to the Quay together. Throughout their lives, the two were always quibbling about the silliest of things. Except for his father, Mihali was the only male in the Alexiou family. And as progressive as the family was in comparison with most in the city, the traditional gender roles were still very much instilled into the children. Celia was never allowed to go to the Quay without her brother. She would walk alone to Anastasia's home or school, but never anywhere outside the Greek Quarter of the city.

Very often, Mihali would try to take charge of all three of his sisters. Anastasia would generally ignore him, depending on how important the issue was. Maria almost always was agreeable towards her brother, especially because he wasn't as demanding of her as he was of her older sisters. Celia found Mihali to be the only male she would challenge. Her confidence in doing so had come almost two years earlier, when Celia had grown taller than her brother. She didn't know it, but it embarrassed Mihali, who worried that she would always tower over him. He would look weak, he thought. But within the last year, he had catapulted into a handsome young man. His dark hair and striking blue eyes had begun to draw the attention of some of Celia's friends.

And as much as he would have liked to have had a brother, he soon became much more approachable to his sisters, especially the one who questioned him the most. Last summer, he and Celia had started coming more often to the Quay, where they would have a variety of discussions. Celia spoke better English than he did, and she engaged in philosophical and socio-economic discussions with him, impressing him.

As they passed the intersection where Celia and Mihali would usually turn to go towards the Quay, the young girl remembered again how hard he had fallen to the ground earlier that morning and she winced at the image of his head hitting the step. Her brother's blood spewed from his handsome face, speckling the white wall. It was the first time Celia had seen someone so violently assaulted.

Tired, and walking as though blind, Celia wondered where he and their father were and if she would ever see them again. However idealistic, she envisioned Mihali and her father finding a way to escape their captors and make their way to the Quay, where she would meet them all. Her mind had begun racing and while the beginning of her imaginary version of reality was hopeful, logic took her to the most frightful outcomes.

Silently, she let two tears fall onto her cheek and hoped the two men would be able to stay together, through whatever they had to endure. The thought of one having to witness the other dying, was agonizing for Celia to imagine. *If one has to die, I hope it's not Mihali. I love Baba. More than anything.* She instantly saw the image of Mihali holding their dying father in his arms, both of them covered in the same dirt that was covering her own shoes. She could see Mihali's tears, and his handsome face wrenched in agony. With that image in her head, the shivers that started in the back of her neck ran down to her shoulders. She stopped them there. *I can't let my imagination think of the worst. Why do I always go to the worst?*

She purposely looked around the street, trying to find something else to focus on. They were in an area of the city where there were more shops and businesses than homes. But they were all closed. Three women appeared from one of the side streets, but they quickly headed for the Quay, not bothering to speak to Celia and her companions. There was no one else. Even the usual stray dogs and cats were nowhere to be seen.

The hush in the streets and dark shadows from the buildings made Celia feel a bit uneasy, but the road was now made of larger setts, bringing a sense of security, knowing they were nearing the Point. She had run out of things to talk about and had given up trying to break the awkward silence. Even the widow was tired of conversing. All they could hear was the faint cries and sounds of chaos coming from the roads around them.

Celia took a moment and looked behind her. She hadn't looked back since she had knocked Voula to the ground. But now, it wasn't just the smoke that was concerning. Far in the distance, she could see hints of flames just above the buildings. The cloud of grey smoke was also wider. *The fire is growing.*

Celia knew Voula couldn't walk any faster, but a sense of urgency was starting to grow within her.

The Quay gradually moved eastward the further north they travelled. The three women were coming closer to it as roads between them and the pier disappeared and the sea became visible between buildings.

They were on Frank Street now and if they stayed on the present route they would eventually find themselves right behind the French Consulate, which was two streets west of the French hospital. Once there, Celia knew they wouldn't be too far from the Point and from the Mr. Lattimore the old man had mentioned. On a regular day, Frank Street would be bustling with movement, but it was eerily quiet, even though Celia saw more and more people walking to the Quay. No one was stopping to chat.

The three women saw two chairs had been thrown onto the street in front of a large building they passed.

"Please, can I sit for a bit?" pleaded Voula. "I can't move any further." She held her back with one hand and reached for a chair with the other. The two women looked at each other and knew they had no choice but to let her. It was that, or they would have to carry her.

Celia picked up the one chair that still had its four legs intact, although it had no back support. Voula moaned as she sat on it. *Her belly is rather large*, Celia thought. Larger than any other she had ever seen. She rarely saw any pregnant women beyond their eighth month, and she couldn't remember what her mother had looked like when she was pregnant with Maria. She had been almost five years old at the time.

Kyria Eleni looked like a woman who was not used to a lot of physical labour, but she was strong. She did not seem arrogant, but had a grand presence, her posture impeccable. She was a woman of few words, but articulate and calm, even though her first words to the teenager had been abrupt. Her waist was thin, and she had narrow hips; as an older woman, she was rather tall, slightly shorter than Celia. Her fine hair was totally white, but nicely cut just below the jaw line. Celia noticed she had a wide wedding band on her right hand. It had some detailing on it, as well, close to its outer edges. Celia had caught a glimpse of her wrinkled hand earlier, as she wiped the sweat off her forehead.

The band caught the sun and reflected it brilliantly for a second, long enough for Celia to notice the woman's delicate hands. They didn't appear to have worked in fields or with livestock. Her black skirt and black blouse—and her grey, dirt-ridden Oxfords, which had once been black—told the teen that the woman was probably a widow. But the fabrics, the style, and just the way the woman carried herself told Celia this woman was well-versed in fashion. Angela was an avid seamstress and had often spoken to her girls about the different types of fabrics, their appropriate uses, their ability to flow or crease, and their varying values.

Kyria Eleni, like most widows, wore a gold crucifix. It was not large, but it looked heavy, as did the chain that held it. At first, Celia wondered how she was still wearing it. The soldiers surely would have ripped such a prize off of her. Then she noticed her blouse had buttons, and her décolletage looked like it had not seen very much sun. The woman, Celia concluded, had probably been covered to her neck when the intruders broke into their home, or she had been hiding somewhere.

Kyria Eleni looked and spoke like a refined woman, one who would make sure she was appropriately dressed even at the crack of dawn. But the hot September sun had now forced everyone to shed some of their extra clothes, such as vests and shawls, and unbutton their shirts and blouses. *That may explain the crucifix. How did she manage to keep her wedding band?*

Celia thought Voula was one of the sweetest young women she had ever met. She spoke with gentle kindness despite her pain and her present situation. And as she sat in the broken chair, Celia wondered how much further the young woman would be able to go.

Voula was only slightly taller than Anastasia, no more than five feet tall, but she had dark wavy hair that fell just past her shoulders and brown, almond-shaped eyes. To look at the pregnant young woman from behind, no one would realize she was expecting. She tried to fan the white cotton blouse that now had turned to beige from the dust. It was quite wide to accommodate her condition and had shorter sleeves than her mother-in-law's blouse, thankfully. The young woman's enlarged belly had lifted the hem of her dark red skirt to show her black sandals and swollen feet, also covered in dust.

She was not wearing her wedding band, Celia noticed, but she could see the pale skin where it had once been, along with a scratch on her finger. Her white blouse was also partially unbuttoned, at times revealing a white camisole, and her white and black straw hat had a wide brim to keep the sun away. Even that was uncomfortable at times, making Voula remove it every so often to use as a fan.

Unlike most of those heading to the Quay, the two women weren't bringing anything from their home. There were no bags, no rugs, no icons in their arms. Celia knew they had left their home quickly because of the soldiers, but the young woman wondered if they even lived in the same home. That would possibly explain why the mother-in-law still had her jewellery, while Voula did not. Their clothing told Celia that this family was probably "more fortunate," than her own, as her mother would say. But even the young girl knew that, currently, in this city, anyone who was Greek, or Armenian was not at all fortunate, regardless of their wealth. In fact, those who were more affluent were the *most* unfortunate, being the most targeted.

Celia's own family was financially comfortable. Her father worked for the Petroleum Company of Smyrna. She didn't know exactly what he did, but she knew it was a clean job, since he always spoke about "his office." His hands were never dirty or calloused when he came home, unlike many of the farmers or even the other workers in the company. Simo made enough money so that three years ago they were able to afford to add a second floor to their home. He always wore a suit to work, even in the summer, and he wore a different shirt every day. It was one of Celia's chores to iron her father's shirts, and Angela made certain to teach her how to do it properly.

Angela would never let Simo leave the house before looking to see if his appearance was perfect. Celia and Anastasia joked one time that if the inspection was Angela's preference or their father's. After her approval was given, he would pick up his hat and leave, announcing his expected time of return. He never left the house without his hat. In the summer it was the white boater hat, and in the winter months, it was the black fedora. It was how most men in the city dressed, particularly the ones who worked in offices or with the public. The Muslim men wore their fez, while all young boys wore a newsboy or flat hat. Simo hadn't switched to the fedora, yet. It was still too warm.

As Voula sat, trying to catch her breath, Celia looked around at her surroundings. She asked Kyria Eleni if she could leave for a few minutes. She showed her where she was going and said she would remain in sight, commenting that there were no signs of soldiers in the vicinity. The widow agreed and kept her eyes on the young girl as she walked away. It was difficult to do, as there were more and more people heading in the same direction as Celia, but even the widow wanted to know what was happening on the waterfront.

Chapter 12

Endurance

Celia walked back towards the intersection they had just passed to get an understanding of where they were in relation to the Point. Again, she looked into the distance, to the south, and the smoke looked to be blowing towards the harbour in the west. The flames, too, but they were also increasing in height. Celia, however, was lost in thought and wasn't concerned with what she was witnessing. She turned the corner, still within Kyria Eleni's sight, and walked towards the Quay. That particular corner was an empty schoolyard, so she could remain relatively visible through the crowd.

Looking down at the two or three feet ahead of her, Celia continued to think about her family. She imagined her father walking in the door, as he did every day from work. He'd call out for Angela as soon as he closed the door behind him, and continue past the small hall, place his hat in his room, and take off his jacket if he hadn't already done so on his walk home. After rolling up his sleeves, he would go into the kitchen, where he would wash his hands and face. Simo would ask what was for dinner, and his wife would tell him. Angela would have dinner prepared and would begin placing it on the table, after hearing Simo come through the front door.

Realizing she was close to tears again, Celia decided to focus on the current situation. Passing the last street before the Quay, she realized she would be lost from the sight of Kyria Eleni and Voula and decided to turn back. But before doing so, she looked up, straight ahead onto the Quay, and saw the multitude of people. The sight confused her, and she took a closer look, crouching her head and squinting her eyes. She couldn't tell how far towards the harbour the crowd went, or how far north or south, but the noise level told her there were more people who she could not see from her vantage point. The image concerned her. There were more people in that immediate vicinity than she could have ever imagined.

We need to keep moving. We won't find a place to sit, she thought to herself. They had to find help for the pregnant woman soon. *I have no idea what to do if this baby comes. Does Kyria Eleni?* Celia was too young to know about birthing, and she had no desire to learn at that moment. Her mind began to race and she consciously tried to keep herself from panicking. *We have to move, but we need to stay calm,* she told herself. She had to get back to the young pregnant woman and her mother-in-law and begin walking for the Point.

In the side street, she saw three men in civilian clothing. All three wore fezzes and were dragging a fourth man in a uniform, a Greek soldier, and very likely the last of those who hadn't made it out of the city. Celia froze. Blood covered the right side of his head and ear and his right arm looked like it had been broken, as it hung in a most peculiar way. Celia's eyes became glazed, but a gunshot elsewhere startled her back to her surroundings. She realized she had to move, but not so quickly as to be noticed by the men. She put her head down and began to head toward the other two women, bumping into someone heading in the opposite direction. The sound of the approaching footsteps brought a flash of sweat across her forehead, but as their sound faded, she sighed with relief.

Celia could see Voula holding her belly. *Maybe by the time this baby is born, the soldiers will have left all our homes, and we can return to them.* Without realizing her actions, Celia put her hand on her own stomach. Between her slight hunger and the image she had just seen, she recognized her queasiness. She also knew that, soon, she'd have to find some way to deal with her monthly nuisance. Just thinking of the usual cramping started to make her anxious. She hated being a woman, but she understood there was no other option than to accept it. She wasn't prepared for it, yet and hoped her body could hold off a few more days.

Her thoughts began to run away again and questioned if she would ever have a child of her own. *Is marriage even a possibility now? Who's left to marry? Can I still become a teacher?* Her parents, especially her father, had told her she could do both, just as Kyria Antigone had. But now was not the time for speculating about the future. All ideas and scenarios were flashing at her randomly and she tried desperately to stop herself from the confusion. She closed her eyes as she approached the two women and, again, told herself to stop panicking.

"Why are you holding your belly, Celia? Is something wrong?" asked Kyria Eleni with concern. Celia was almost startled by the tone in her voice. It brought her back to reality and out of her own head.

"Oh, I am okay, Kyria Eleni. I am just thinking about what day this is, but I'm okay for now," said Celia, with the look of annoyance teen girls often adopt when irked. Knowing what happens to women during times of war and conflict, Kyria Eleni seemed relieved when she realized what was on the young woman's mind.

With nothing more to talk about, and Voula looking like she was not ready to budge yet, again, Celia's imagination returned to the multiple scenarios about her family.

Mihali and I would have been to the Quay and back by now. But poor Voula could not walk fast and trying to keep a pregnant woman up was tiresome. Maybe she should have stayed with her family, she thought. Celia missed her mother terribly, her sisters, too, and hoped they had made it to the Quay by now.

How could I have been so hurtful to Mama? Her mind had shifted to the remnants of her family, and she caught herself feeling a deep sense of guilt. She was so concerned about these strangers, but not enough about her own mother and sisters, she thought. She began to feel she had abandoned them in order to help these two women. *It was hubris. Who did I think I was fooling by pretending to be so smart, so capable? No, I will not cry!*

She leaned her back on the gate behind Voula's chair. Her curly hair was falling in her face, and she tried to blow it away, bringing her jaw outwards. But it went nowhere, except further into her eyes. *Oh, for heaven's sake! Even my hair has become an enemy now!* The sweat held some of it where it could frustrate her even more. Irritated, she grabbed her curls and furiously stuck them back in the ponytail. Celia became so caught in her own creation of chaos, she wanted to jump out of her skin. Her knees became weak, and she struggled to breathe, feeling suffocated by the heat.

An overwhelming sense of exhaustion poured from her emotional turmoil, and despite the stifling heat, the warmth of the gate on her back was a pleasing sensation. It was almost one o'clock and Celia knew the worst of the heat was yet to come. She grabbed the gate's metal rods behind her, trying not to look distressed in front of the strangers. Celia could feel her nails digging into her palms and knew she had to keep herself from losing control.

She consciously calmed herself down, dropping her shoulders and staring up into the sky where a barn swallow was gliding past her. Its beautiful blue feathers were caught in the wind, sparing it from working for its flight, if only for a few seconds, and allowing it to witness images it probably had never seen before in its short life. The young woman wished she could follow it towards hibernation. *How lucky you are,* she whispered to the bird high above.

Celia hadn't realized how tired she was, how far she had walked, almost forgetting the other two were with her. Her head still leaning back onto the gate, looking into the skies, Celia watched the swallow disappear to the south and took a big breath. *Please God, hear me, hear all of us, who need You now.* She scanned the heavens to see if there was a sign anywhere from Him. The Being she heard about throughout her short life should make his appearance soon, give some sort of sign telling everyone she saw on the Quay that help was on its way. She always wondered where He was, why no one could ever see Him. She wondered how He would finally appear…*would he send ships with Greek soldiers? Would he strike down the enemy with a ball of fire? Would he make it rain to send people the water and relief they needed?* But the only thing that changed as she looked up, was that one more tear fell from her brown eyes. As startled as she was when Kyria Eleni put her hand on her shoulder, it was a welcome touch of tenderness.

"My girl, shed your tears. We have all earned the right to do so. But the sooner you realize that tears won't help us, the faster you will overcome your pain. Strength and wile are what we need. Men are physically stronger, and they know it, but guile is something they cannot see coming from a woman. They always say we're cunning, but they don't always believe it. They underestimate our intelligence."

Celia was captivated by the widow's words. She believed this woman to be sharp and resourceful, but something told her the widow had a mysterious history. As she looked at Kyria Eleni, she noticed how her white hair and grey eyes softened the woman's entire being. Celia felt somehow hypnotized by her. The delicate nature of the older woman contrasted with the strength in her voice and the design of her words. Celia stood up and away from the gate, nodding in agreement with Kyria Eleni.

She's right. It's strength I need now, she told herself, *and God already gave me that when he created me.* That's what her father would tell her. Whenever Celia was conflicted about something, he would remind her that God had already graciously given her tools. She just needed to figure out how to use them.

Resting only four buildings away from the north corner, the three women saw another wave of people walking west, towards the harbour. It was a parade like the one outside Celia's home. But these people were different. All of them had a look of desperation and weariness. Some had blood on their clothes and swollen injuries on their bodies. They were dirty, completely covered in dust. Some were bruised, some cut, and others walked with a stick or cane, regardless of their age. Many of the older men were walking without shirts, revealing their sagging, aged skin. It was pale white, as very few of them had bared their chests to the passing summer's rays.

Celia could see most of them still wearing their hats and holding a white handkerchief to wipe the sweat off their faces. Initially, Celia couldn't understand why most of the men were barefoot. But then it came to her: if they were going to be stopped by anyone on the road, it would be other men—men who had no interest in women's shoes.

One family had managed to carry their belongings on a cart, which was pulled by a young boy and an old man on one side, and a woman on the other. The cart was overloaded, as Celia could see the middle was warping. Two little girls in identical dresses and pigtails walked with them as well. The twins looked down at their feet as they shuffled and had sullen looks on their dirty faces. Every so often their mother would call to them to keep up with their family and then, soon enough, they would fall behind again.

Most of the refugees carried suitcases or large bags. Household items could be seen in the crowd, as well. Rugs, pans, a spinning wheel, even a sewing machine went by on another cart. Further down the line, two young women were struggling to help a third, much older, woman. The old woman seemed barely conscious as she tried to keep her head upright. Her arms were draped around the necks of the two girls and their arms in turn were awkwardly wrapped around her torso. It was evident that the two younger women had been carrying this woman for a while because they had almost mastered a carefully synchronized walk. The old woman looked tiny; the years had eaten away at her shrinking bones. Kyria Eleni saw them, quietly scoffed and shook her head.

"Even if she is their mother, it would be better to let the woman go so she knows she is no longer a burden to them." Celia turned sharply to her with a puzzled look.

"It is harsh to say, I know, Celia. But these barbarians will never stop until every Greek and Armenian is out of this city. And our barbarians will never stop trying to take back what was once ours. And mark my words, the Jews will be next. They'll want them out of the city, soon enough."

The mother-in-law's words were sharp and her grey eyes were widened but almost glassy. Frustration was growing within her, and she looked up at the blue sky and shook her head again. She, too, decided to lean on the warm gate, exhausted. The wrinkled part of her neck was stretched now, almost hiding her years. But her cheeks, which had once been rosy and firm, still drooped next to the outlines of her full lips. As Celia stared at the widow, it became obvious to her that Kyria Eleni had once been a very beautiful woman.

"So, it will never end," said Celia with a sense of hopelessness in her voice, turning to watch the old woman in the procession, whose head was now hanging back as she and her escorts disappeared behind the stone building on the corner.

"Not as long as women give birth to soldiers," said Kyria Eleni. "But can we live without soldiers, without war? Let's hope not because that's when men will have little use for us. They cannot create armies by themselves." Kyria Eleni's voice turned somber and sympathetic. She looked to Celia and said, "I saw your sister's face. People think that only men die in battle. But they are only the ones whose bodies are counted and buried."

Celia looked to the ground as her lips widened, not to smile but to confirm what the woman was correct in her words. *Where is my sister now?* she wondered. As she started recreating the look on Anastasia's face in the bedroom, she just as quickly shut it from her mind. She was the most beautiful bride. *She was always so good to me*, she told herself, instead. When she looked up again to the crowd, something caught her attention, and her big brown eyes widened. Her mouth dropped open, and she gasped.

"Look!" shouted Celia, as she pointed into the crowd, where two women were stopping the people coming from the east who looked sick or unable to continue. As they were dressed in white, the teenager realized that the women were nurses. One of them wore a large black sun hat, similar to the one worn by the widow next to her. Kyria Eleni couldn't see them immediately, but before she could figure out what the young girl was pointing to, Celia was running towards the crowd.

The young girl picked up her skirt, revealing long graceful legs that managed to run through the parade of souls without touching a single passerby. The older woman squinted to see and when she finally did, her left hand covered her mouth, her right made a sign of a cross over her shoulders and chest, and she then bent down to hug Voula.

Chapter 13

Angels in White

Celia quickly and effortlessly ebbed through the flagging crowd of people who barely noticed her and grabbed the arm of the taller, plumper nurse. Her dark brown and greying hair was pulled back, revealing the onset of wrinkles next to her eyes and thin lips. With furrowed brows, Kyria Eleni watched as the woman looked in the direction Celia was pointing and then turned to the other nurse.

They spoke to each other, and the shorter one darted quickly forward towards the Quay, running past the refugees who were heading that way, too. Celia and the other nurse headed straight for Celia's companions. With tears of joy, Kyria Eleni brought her hands together as if in prayer, letting out a sigh of relief.

"It won't be long, my child. Celia found a nurse," said Kyria Eleni. "Please be patient, help is coming."

Relieved at the news, Voula just nodded and held her belly. She could not speak, and finally had to release the gush of tears that could no longer be contained. She began to sob, putting her hands to her face. Her mother-in-law tried to console her, but poor Voula knew what lay ahead for her and her child. Sitting in the heat, on a half-broken chair was the limit of her patience and hope. She unleashed the anguish and could not stop, no matter how much Kyria Eleni pleaded with her.

By the time the teen and the nurse got to Voula, the young mother-to-be was inconsolable. The nurse immediately bent down and held the shoulders of the young pregnant woman.

"Entaxi, entaxi," said the nurse, as she rubbed Voula's arms. Her Greek was very broken, but using a hand gesture, she introduced herself as Jane DeBlanc. She managed to calm Voula enough to bring the sobbing down to whimpers. The nurse was curt, but empathetic.

"She needs to calm down, both for her own, and her baby's welfare. Please translate what's about to happen," she said to Celia. Jane's crusty demeanour did not intimidate the young woman. She only nodded and waited for instructions. "Tell her I have sent for a car to take her to the Dutch hospital. A nurse will accompany her. When she arrives at the hospital, a Dr. Preston will be there to help her."

Celia explained this to Voula and Kyria Eleni, who turned to the nurse and asked in Greek if she could go with her daughter-in-law. The mother-in-law's hand gestures and Jane's limited understanding of the language, told her what she was saying without Celia having to interpret.

"Tell her, I do not know for certain, but most likely, yes," said Jane. Celia did so. Kyria Eleni' looked up to the sky and her eyes filled with tears; she breathed another sigh of relief. After making the sign of the cross again, she hugged Voula, and, for the first time since they had met, Celia saw a smile break onto the older woman's face. Her eyes beamed and new life exuded from them, like a child just given a brand-new toy. *Yes, she had once been a very beautiful woman, this Kyria Eleni*, thought Celia.

"You should come with us, too," said Kyria Eleni, gently laying her hand on Celia's forearm. "I don't want you to go on without finding someone to go with you, back to your mother." The older woman's offer was unexpected, and her warmth touched Celia.

"What is she saying?" asked Jane.

"I'm supposed to go back to the Quay. My mother and sisters are there, but she doesn't want me to go alone. She wants me to go with her and Voula."

"I understand, but I doubt you will be allowed in the hospital. It's very full, my dear. It's likely you will be told to leave, and the hospital is between the Greek and Armenian Quarters. I don't think it's a good idea to be walking there alone," said the nurse remorsefully. "You can come with me and help us at the safehouse. Hopefully, Mr. Lattimore or one of the American sailors might be able to help find your family. You'll be closer to them, as well."

"If you come with us, Celia, you may be able to get on a boat faster," protested the older Greek woman, who realized the nurse didn't sound encouraging.

"I have a French passport and gold coins with me. I can buy us tickets to Piraeus or maybe even France. I know it may be without your family, but at least you have a better chance to get out of the city." Kyria Eleni continued trying to convince Celia.

"My dear, I have heard they will not let Greeks and Armenians board the foreign ships," she added. "People have been on the Quay for days, unable to leave. The other governments don't want to jeopardize their relationship with Kemal and the new regime so they will not permit people on board. And they won't let Greek ships into the harbour to take the refugees, either. I also know that the government in Greece is about to fall, so we can't expect much from them. You've seen the buildings. The city has shut down and soon people won't have access to food and water. Those on the waterfront are already suffering." Celia was shocked. The widow spoke like a diplomat or politician. A general, even. She wasn't emotional, just confident about what she knew.

"I'll tell them you are my daughter, and we don't have papers for you. That we left them behind when the soldiers told us to leave our house. I'll coach you until we speak to them, so that our stories are the same, and I'll even teach you some French. I am very good at negotiating." While she sounded well-acquainted with what was happening and seemed to know how to accomplish her task, Kyria Eleni's concern for the young girl was evident.

Celia was humbled by the offer, but shocked by Kyria Eleni's knowledge and craftiness. The young woman was overwhelmed by everything she had just heard. But even if she could eventually get out of the city, Jane told her she probably wouldn't be able to stay in the Dutch hospital, which would be the girl's first hurdle.

The young teen's head was still spinning from confusion as they heard the black car in the distance. She saw the vehicle approach them and wondered if she should ignore the nurse's words and push her way inside to join Voula and Kyria Eleni.

As it came to a stop, the passenger door opened and the other nurse she had seen earlier, stepped out. At the same time, the driver, a man, got out of the car, too. The young nurse turned to him and motioned him to get back into the car. He did not reply to her but did what she told him. She looked like she was in her early thirties, and she was a beautiful woman with green eyes and red hair pulled back into a bun. Her small, delicate frame did not match her movement. Her eyes focused immediately on the young woman in the chair, and she marched towards her.

"Voula, this is Maisie Lane," said Jane. She knew Voula didn't speak English, but she knew the English introduction would be understood. Maisie, smiling, put her hands under Voula's arms to help her up. With Kyria Eleni and Celia helping as well, the young woman got up and Maisie very gently pushed Celia aside, slipping her arm around Voula's waist. She guided her to the car, pointed to the rear passenger door, and opened it for her.

Celia immediately felt a sense of loss when Maisie took over helping Voula. She stepped back and stood next to Jane. As much as she wanted to get in that car, Celia realized that she couldn't. It would be too tight for the three of them to sit in the back seat and to force her way into the car was simply uncharacteristic of her. Besides, she desperately wanted to meet her family at the consulate on the Quay.

She watched Kyria Eleni and Maisie gently help Voula up and into the back seat where she plopped, wincing. The widow looked at Celia as she walked around the car to get to the other passenger door, waiting for a sign. Neither spoke to each other.

"Maisie," called out Jane. "Look." Maisie turned to look at her colleague, who was pointing at the chair where Voula was sitting. Celia looked, too. It was wet, she noticed, as was the dirt underneath the chair. Celia was surprised at the sight and wondered if Voula had peed herself.

"Her water has broken," said Jane. "I hope Dr. Preston is at the hospital when you get there."

"I hope so, too!" called out Maisie, as she closed the door to the car. She sat in the front with the driver and Kyria Eleni sat next to Voula in the back. The car left immediately, without anyone exchanging goodbyes and well wishes.

Celia saw the dust rise from the wheels as the car pulled away and headed back towards the direction the women had come from. Kyria Eleni turned and waved to Celia, who waved back at the mysterious widow. The drive would involve going through the Greek and Armenian neighbourhoods, where Celia knew the soldiers were still roaming. But just as the old man close to her home had said, the American flag was on the car and that gave Celia some reassurance.

Celia would have kept her eyes on the disappearing car, had she not realized how intense the smell of the smoke had just become. The breeze had picked up and brought the reality of the situation back to her. In the far distance, beyond the remnants of the dust the vehicle had stirred, she could see soldiers banging on someone's door. *How can it be safe to go back there,* she wondered. She looked at Jane and the nurse put her hand on Celia's shoulder.

"Let's get to the safehouse, Celia. There are plenty of people who can use our help." Celia was more than happy to do so, wanting to be as far away from the soldiers as possible.

Chapter 14

Time to Leave

Charles Brice inspected the city every day. And although he was not the captain of the *USS Lawrence*, he was the most senior officer in Smyrna. By September 13th the Quay had been turned into a giant terminal of people going nowhere. There were tens of thousands of refugees and the situation had become critical. In recent days, many of the city's Christians had begun coming to the Quay, hearing the horrible rumours of Kemal's army in the countryside. Others thought that there would be another period of transition, as there had been in the past, a time where it would be unfortunate to be Greek or Armenian, as it had been before 1919. But by that morning, all Christians in Smyrna knew the Turks were not interested in co-existence. They wanted them out of the city or dead.

If there were any Greek soldiers in or close to Smyrna, they had changed into civilian clothing; others had left for less conspicuous sea access points, hoping to escape detention by Turks who had begun actively looking for them in the crowds. Turkish civilians, specifically males, had also become threatening and even engaged in barbaric behaviour against the refugees, knowing there would be no repercussions. Theft, assault, and murder were rampant in the city, specifically on the Quay and the roads leading to the Greek and Armenian Quarters.

The representatives of all the foreign governments were now spectators in this region of the world and the only thing to could consider was their future relationship with the side that was left standing. Some nations had already moved past the prejudices of the World War and were selling weapons to Kemal's army. It was now 1922 and however noble it would be to support a Christian group of people, keeping themselves agreeable to the new incoming government of this region was the more profitable stand to take.

Even though it would take almost a century to be acknowledged, what was unfolding in Smyrna was part of a genocide that had already been developing in the northern part of the country, primarily against the Armenians. And, as the American consul of the city, Stephen Herman was aware of it all. But Admiral Boyd determined much of American policy in Asia Minor, and the consul was almost as helpless as those in the harbour.

Acknowledging that a show of force must be reserved for Americans and American properties, the American Naval officers agreed to post guards at major American businesses and agencies. Marines stood at the Standard Oil Company, a carpet company, the American Girls' School, the YWCA, and the YMCA. The British had already advised all their nationals to leave the city, and two days earlier, Herman had sent word to a number of Americans whose presence in Smyrna could prove to be dangerous. He had advised them to leave as soon as possible and all of them were already in the harbour, on the *USS Litchfield*.

Brice met Stephen Herman at the American consulate at noon, as usual. The two marines guarding the building allowed only ten people inside, at a time. Brice entered and, removing his hat, looked for the consul. Herman appeared from his office wearing a short-sleeved white shirt, without his jacket or tie. He looked tired and his cane seemed to shake as he leaned on it. He motioned Brice to go outside, hoping to find some fresh air. Brice obliged him, opening the door for the man and walking only a few feet from the entrance, away from the queue that stretched to the next block. Brice looked out into the harbour.

"One has a different perspective from this side of the water, don't you think, Captain?" asked Herman. The sixty-year-old took out a white handkerchief and wiped the sweat that had clumped small tufts of his grey hair to his forehead and the sides of his head, above his ears.

"Indeed."

"I heard a French official was murdered yesterday. I don't know if it was a soldier or some Turkish rabble, but it's not the peaceful transition Kemal's general had promised. Especially when I'm seeing bodies lining the streets, Captain Brice." Herman was visibly frustrated. Brice had also seen what was happening on the Quay and in the rest of Smyrna. In the three days he had been in the city, his sympathy towards the refugees had increased dramatically. Yet, he had no intentions of offering any more support than had already been given. Admiral Boyd would end his career without hesitation.

"I have seen them, too, Mr. Herman." Brice offered nothing more.

"I've also had reports that the fire, now raging in the Armenian Quarter, was deliberately set. Reporters and others loyal to Admiral Boyd and Kemal have said it's Greeks and Armenians who started it. Everyone else, I mean *everyone* else, people who have actually witnessed the fires ignited by someone, have said it was Turks."

Brice, glaring into the harbour and breathing more heavily, remained quiet.

Realizing the captain had nothing more to offer, Herman announced his intentions.

"I am reaching out to *all* Americans to evacuate the city as soon as possible, Captain. I have spoken to the officers of the *USS Litchfield* and the *USS Simpson*. They are receiving US nationals as we speak. Most of them are missionaries or the families of businessmen and officials, but I hope to get *everyone* out by tonight.

"Yes, Mr. Herman, I've been advised of such. As a senior officer, I have been contacted by the other officers of those ships and I have already informed those on the *Lawrence* that we may be evacuating American civilians."

"Very good, Captain. I wanted to be sure you were aware. I know what our government's policy is with respect to the refugees. But, Captain, if you can influence or encourage the powers that be to evacuate these people, these *Christians*, please do so. This will not end well, otherwise."

Brice stared at the consul general and slowly nodded. Herman waited for words and before he could continue with his agenda, Brice showed himself.

"Mr. Herman, I see what is happening, I mean, *really* happening, and so do my men." Brice scrunched over a little and squinted as he whispered.

"I am constantly bombarded by their emotions every time they come ashore, more than I have ever experienced, and I try to remind them, they are *not* civilians or nannies, they are servicemen for the United States Navy." Brice began to snip and raise his voice, but Herman remained calm.

"I am desperately trying to keep them from compromising themselves or our country! Sir!" The captain glared at Herman, who understood the pressure Brice was under and knew that as much as he had tried with the other captains, as well, Brice was not going to bend for the refugees. In him, as in the others, shame was stirring. Herman stared at the captain and sighed.

"Well, I'll let you return to your ship, Captain. We both have much work to do. "

"Thank you, Mr. Herman," snapped Brice.

As Captain Brice put his hat back on his head, and turned to walk away, Herman tried one more time.

"Then please prepare yourself, Captain. Because based on what I am seeing, I believe there will be very few Americans or otherwise that will want to remain in this city, or even return. I can only imagine what horrors of war you have seen in your lifetime. But not everyone knows how to live with them, sir."

Brice stopped to listen, lowering his head. But he didn't turn around to face Herman. He looked back out towards the ships in the harbour and headed straight for the whaleboat.

Chapter 15

The Hero, Mr. Lattimore

Celia and Jane continued to walk north towards the Point. The young girl had become so overwhelmed, she was starting to get a headache. It wasn't a long walk. Celia would walk this route in less than an hour on a normal day. But the heat, the feeling of uncertainty, and the underestimated effort needed to keep Voula upright had exhausted her. Recognizing the signs of dehydration, Jane tried to do most of the talking.

She told Celia about the places she had been called to work, such as Paris and Prague. She was single and originally from Detroit and was now the director of nursing for the Near East Relief in Constantinople. She had experience not only working in extreme battlefield situations, but she also trained many young women to become nurses.

Her white skirt and blouse showed signs of blood in some areas and the long skirt's hem was almost black from the dirt. Most of Jane's greying brown hair had been pulled back under her broad-brimmed black hat, and her forehead was drenched in sweat, beading just above her thick eyebrows. She wasn't the most attractive of women, but her brown eyes were soft, balancing her authoritative nature just enough to be approachable.

"The safehouse is not far, Celia," Jane said to the teenager, who was relieved to hear it. The thirst was pulling at her throat when she swallowed. Sweat had drenched her blouse under her jacket. It was her light jacket, fortunately, but it was still an added layer of clothing that was not necessary for this heat. A few times, she was tempted to remove it, but she worried she would either drop it or someone would very easily grab it from her hands, especially while she was helping Voula. While it was almost negligible in weight, Celia could swear she was carrying another fifteen pounds.

She thought of Kyria Eleni, who had told her she had some of her own coins and wondered if they were sewn into her skirt or just sitting in her stuffed purse. It didn't surprise her that the widow had money. She smiled and gave herself some praise for being able to recognize the woman's affluence.

Celia was feeling a sense of separation from the two women she had known for less than two hours. She was grateful for Kyria Eleni's offer. Realistically, Celia really didn't know how much gold the woman had in her purse. Her real concern was whether she did the right thing in not taking an opportunity which might never present itself again. She didn't know how many gold coins it would take for her family to flee the city. And what they would do if they did not have enough.

Celia's preoccupation made her ignore Jane's direction to turn left at the intersecting streets they had just come to. She also didn't realize that a group of refugees had also been coming through that street, walking towards the Quay. When she almost bumped into a woman, and then heard Jane's sharp call, she startled out of her daze. She looked around to take notice of where she was. *What am I doing?* asked Celia, scolding herself aloud.

"Celia!" called out the nurse. "This way. Please stay close to me." The teen looked up and saw Jane's stern look on her pouting face, and quickly caught up to her.

Her sense of smell was immediately jolted as she took the turn and looked up to find the source from the Quay. It wasn't intense, but it was very new to her, and quite offensive. Normally, the Quay's more unpleasant odours would come from the ships. But as it was still early in the day, freshly baked goods would also normally be permeating the harbourfront. Tiropites and spanakopites, crepes, baguettes, kouloures, and touloumbes would be ready for purchase at the bakeries and patisseries on or near the Quay. Now, even the smells of the sea and the smoke had been overpowered by the scent of human suffrage.

It was then that Celia remembered an argument she and Mihali had had with their mother a few days earlier. Angela was furious that they had planned to go to the Quay. This was the reason, Celia now realized. Kyria Eleni said that people had been on the Quay for days. The snippets of chatter the teenager had been hearing lately always included mention of the Quay, but it was only now that she understood why. The widow was right ... *people have already been suffering,* she said to herself.

In fact, people had been flocking to the city for weeks, but Angela and Simo had tried to keep their children from seeing the accumulation of refugees coming from the surrounding towns and villages. Refugees who did not have family or friends to stay with in Smyrna ended up on the waterfront, waiting to get away. And as families walked towards Smyrna, the able-bodied men, and any valuables, were taken. People were beaten, women ripped away from their loved ones, some later released, some killed. Those who were released had to continue their journeys alone, where they would often fall victim to more attacks.

Celia was awestruck when they reached the Quay. As she and Jane turned right toward the Point, she stared to her left into the harbour. All she could see was the crowd that had gathered on the waterfront and the thin horizontal band of the faraway Aegean Sea. Typically, the *only* thing to be seen beyond the pier was the open sea and some ships. Her earlier glance at the waterfront had not given her the full scope of the situation. She noticed the American Theatre ahead and realized that the French consulate was behind them.

Instantly, Celia forgot her exhaustion and thirst. The vast number of people on the street was more than she had ever seen, more than she imagined she could ever see. Her head stretched as far north and as far south as possible, and the only thing in her line of sight was a horde of bodies. She looked for the French flag, hoping that her mother and sisters would be close, but she knew that even if she could see the flag, she certainly wouldn't have been able to distinguish anyone in the crowd.

"Miss DeBlanc, can we please turn around and go see if my mother and sisters are at the French consulate? It's where I am supposed to meet them and it's only a few buildings away," said Celia, as she reached for the nurse's arm. She was visibly apprehensive about asking the woman to change her plans. Jane raised her eyebrows and lowered her chin at the young girl's request.

"Celia, I understand your desire to be with your family right now, but you don't even know if they're there. And as you can see, there's so many people on this Quay that it would be completely hopeless to look for *anyone* at the moment. Our time would be better spent at the safehouse."

Jane scoffed and before Celia could respond, the nurse began walking towards the north again. The mere seconds lost in order to comment on the subject seemed to aggravate the nurse. Poor Celia felt silly for even asking the question, and quickly followed her.

"As I mentioned earlier," continued Jane, "Mr. Lattimore or some other man may be able to escort you to the French consulate to search for your family, but I cannot."

"Yes, Miss DeBlanc," replied Celia. She coughed, not realizing that smoke had subtly seeped into the breeze. The brief sense of relief had shrouded what was coming next. People everywhere could be heard coughing.

The two women continued to dodge people in their way, with Jane focused on the road ahead, while Celia was distracted by the people on the waterfront. Like the parades of people she had already witnessed, most of them were women and children, with very few men. Those who were of military age did their best to stay out of sight. Celia didn't know whether to be concerned for those men or resentful. She caught glimpses of some who were smoking, silently admonishing them for drawing attention to themselves.

She now understood why her mother took the woven mats in the kitchen. People had laid mats on the ground and were sitting on them, keeping themselves from becoming an extension of the stone and dirt. It was one of the last symbols of civility that separated human beings from dogs and other animals that were walking, defecating, and eating off these streets.

And, yes, there were all sorts of animals in the crowd, besides the usual stray dogs and cats. People from the countryside had brought their chickens, goats, and lambs. And their horses and donkeys drew the carts that carried whatever household items they thought they could salvage for future use, regardless of where they would end up. The waterfront also had rails, as well, evidence of Smyrna's advancements in infrastructure. But there were no trolleys to be seen now.

The animals looked more exhausted and dehydrated than the people. *Where did they think they were taking these poor creatures,* thought the young woman. *Did they not realize they would need food and water, too?* Jane grabbed the young girl by the arm and told her to stay close, so they didn't become separated. Celia was more than happy to comply and moved her arm to grab the nurse by the hand. She began to squint, with her shoulders slightly raised, as she watched the images in front of her.

Most people were standing or walking around aimlessly looking for loved ones or answers to their questions. Celia was too shocked to notice her heart starting to beat faster and her clothing becoming stickier. *With so many people on the Quay, how on earth will I be able to find my family?* she thought to herself. Neither Celia nor her mother had imagined there would be this many people on the street when she had promised to look for them after helping Voula and Kyria Eleni. *If Mama knew this, she never would have let me come. And I wouldn't have wanted to, either,* she told herself.

Celia looked towards the harbour and took note of the many ships there. They were so far away! And there were only three small boats in between them and the pier. *Why are the ships anchored so far in the distance and why are so few boats coming to shore?* she wondered. She noticed one of the small boats had five or six people in it, and it was heading out to sea. *With thousands on the Quay, why were so few being taken out to a ship?* Her furrowed eyebrows revealed her confusion, but no one could give her an explanation.

The only sight of normalcy that caught Celia's attention were the birds in the harbour. Sea gulls had nowhere to wander on the Quay, but they glided smoothly past the ships and boats, as if to poke those aboard into looking beyond the safety of the floating sanctuaries.

Even the great cormorant went about his business, diving for his meal of the day. It was far in the distance, but Celia recognized it. She was always fascinated by the bird, counting to see how long it could remain underwater as it foraged. No matter how much she understood that a cormorant could remain submerged for a long time, she always breathed a sigh of relief when it returned to the surface. This time, she couldn't keep her eyes on the creature because of the many people blocking her view. But she continued to watch for it, and after her count of twelve seconds she could scarcely see its yellow throat patch as it emerged from the sea. But it didn't stay long. Almost immediately, the bird's dark wings stretched wide, and it glided across the water heading inland toward the northeast.

The further north the two women walked along the Quay, the more pitiful the people looked. This was where those from the countryside had first converged. Celia had seen a few of them two months ago, but she wondered if they could possibly be the same people. *Were they?* she wondered. They resembled the beggars that would be found in the more impoverished sections of the city. But some of those now sitting in the northern part of the Quay had once been successful business owners and farmers in their villages. Animals, carts, blankets, and farming tools were evidence that they had begun their journey far from Smyrna. Their gaunt sun-scorched faces, dirty clothes, and cracked lips made it obvious that they had been outdoors for a very long time.

As Celia looked at them, she realized the first people she had seen, in the southern part of the Quay, were cleaner; the women were dressed more fashionably, most wearing hats—some even carrying parasols to protect themselves from the sun. The refugees in the south also didn't look as worn as the people closer to the safehouse, where the stench was worse. There were more possessions in the north, as well, more crates, more animals, more things of use, while the mainly-women population in the south clearly had left their homes quickly. Although the soldiers had harassed those coming from the rural areas as well, many men had managed to enter the city, unseen.

Celia couldn't help but stare at the very few young-to-middle-aged men in the crowd. She wondered how they had managed to get there when so many others had been arrested. *They must have heard of the oncoming soldiers and run to the Quay to escape,* she thought to herself. Celia couldn't know that some of the women were actually men dressed in disguise.

Parents were holding their children, and almost every other adult was holding some household possessions ... holding them as if ready to fight for them if anyone dared to take them, whether it was a child or just a pot. The little ones whimpered, cried even, some adults too. The variety of emotions that people carried with them were not difficult to distinguish. Exhaustion, fear, and pain were most evident. Some had scowling faces and pursed lips. Those whose faces were expressionless were the most frightful. Celia heard quite a few parents scolding their children out of frustration. One grandfather slapped his young grandson across the boy's bum for not sitting on the four-by-four-foot rug.

When sudden yelling caught her attention, Celia saw two women, each pulling on a kitchen mat, both claiming it to be their own. One let go of the mat and reached for the other woman's hair and the argument quickly became more physical. People in the immediate vicinity tried to interject and separate the women, but Jane and Celia continued on their task. Celia looked at them, all, and could only feel lost and distressed. She didn't realize her grip on Jane's hand had tightened.

The crowd was waiting for something or someone to tell them what to do and where to go next. But no one was going anywhere further than five or ten feet. Country folk pushed in from the north and the urbanites came from the south. But now, the mass of people had nowhere to go, nowhere to push. The ones who were moving were the ones who had just arrived. And they couldn't go very far. They had to push their way into the mob from the side streets they had just come from and try to find a place to sit ... and wait.

As Celia and Jane weaved through the mob, they passed two more women. One was holding the forearm of the other who was clutching a child of no more than six months. Celia heard the woman telling the mother that she had to let it go, "it died yesterday." Celia looked at the child and saw that it was pale and lifeless. Gasping, her eyes almost popped out of her head, while her arms and legs felt like molten lava, seeping into the earth. Her flinch caused her to bump into Jane, who grabbed the girl by the shoulders and pulled her towards a door.

Chapter 16

The Safehouse at 490

Jane opened the door and ushered her young companion inside the safehouse. The smell immediately seized Celia. Sweat and blood infused the air, causing her to cough. It was shocking to her that the odour was worse inside than it was on the Quay. She quickly fixed her shrivelled nose when she realized she stood on the most beautiful mosaic floor she had ever seen.

The work of art depicted dolphins and crabs, and even a jellyfish whose image was made of tiny light blue glass pieces. They were the same as those that outlined the entire hallway, as far into the back of the hallway as Celia could see. The outer section of the blue glass mosaic was finished by a rope motif made of gold leaf tesserae and white marble, while in the centre of the hall were more gold-leaf tesserae in the form of the sun.

Looking into the two rooms to the left and right of her, Celia saw young mothers holding infants and women who were clearly going to be giving birth in the next few weeks. She stepped into the room on the left, where there must have been forty or fifty women and children. They were standing, lying in makeshift beds, and sitting on chairs; three new mothers sat next to each other on a long lavishly embroidered sofa, holding their newborns and clumsily trying to nurse them. While Celia could see children sitting with their mothers, something told her that some of them were sitting with strangers who had kindly offered to care for the lost or orphaned little ones.

Celia's eyes were wide as she took inventory of all that surrounded her. Looking past the images of misery, her head turned up to the walls and ceiling of the safehouse. Pictures or paintings that had once hung on the walls were missing, their outlines revealed by the faded paint. The royal blue velvet curtains were pushed against the walls, their muted gold tassels now tangled and torn. Few pieces of furniture sat in the room, obviously removed to make space for the mass of people moving about. *This was probably the sitting room or sala,* Celia thought to herself.

Walking slowly back out of the room and with her jaw slightly ajar, Celia became dizzy looking up at the magnificent metal chandelier that hung above her, just above the gold tesserae sun of the mosaic below. She glanced back into the sala and noticed further in the back there was a similar, but smaller one in what had probably once been a dining room. The sideboard or *servan* against the far wall, told Celia as much. Although two short walls separated the two rooms, Celia did not know that they contained pocket doors that had been retracted into the walls to create more room and circulate the air. While this was not a popular feature even in the more affluent homes of the region, the doctor had seen it in his visits to London and made certain to have it in his home.

No one had removed the Persian rugs in any of the rooms. But only traces of them could be seen under the blankets and sheets that were laid out, stretching out onto the marble floors, to create temporary beds. Very few had pillows, but rolled up clothing lay where it could support a weary head. As she approached a staircase, Celia could hear more women upstairs. Standing by the metal bannister, she tried to take a quick survey of the size of the house and the number of people inside it.

In the back of the house, a familiar scream began and stopped in intervals. Someone was giving birth. Another woman's voice could also be heard saying "a little more, you're almost done," in Greek.

"Have some water, my dear," said Jane as she handed Celia a full glass. She had walked away from Celia, who hadn't even noticed her absence. The nurse had become softer, more agreeable since arriving at the safehouse. "Do not drink it too fast." But Celia had already begun gulping. What she really wanted to do was pour the remaining water over her head. She knew water was scarce, though, and would not dream of doing such a thing. She drank it, with gratitude.

"Come with me," said Jane. Her authoritative tone didn't seem to concern Celia, who tended to be an accommodating person.

Celia left her glass on a small table in the foyer and followed Jane up the stairs where it was even warmer, but the smell was different. She primarily smelled sweat here, and quickly realized she could recognize the difference between it and blood. Celia counted five rooms, and they were all on the north and east sides of the building.

The first two rooms each had two brass beds and large, elaborately decorated armoires; there were approximately twenty women in each of them but none of them looked pregnant.

The faces that weren't hidden under a bedsheet or nestled into their knees, or on a nearby shoulder, wore pain and loss. Their eyelids were drooping, as were the sides of their lips. But their eyes, no matter the colour or shape, looked moribund, almost lifeless. They looked like Anastasia.

In the first room, one girl was sitting in a chair close to a window. Most of the others looked to be no more than age twenty or so. It was almost silent in that room, with some women holding each other, some staring into empty space. A few of them had fallen asleep on the floor, while others just lay awake, curled in a fetal position.

In the other room, Celia slightly gasped at one woman who had been beaten so badly her face was entirely swollen. A young woman next to her was sniffling, obviously crying, and her arm was wrapped in a makeshift sling, while her other arm was holding her abdomen as she rocked back and forth. The rest were either consoling each other or sitting with the familiar dazed and hollow looks on their faces. Their eyes had caught either a knot in the wooden plank on the floor, or the design of the rug, and they had chosen to stare at it, without a blink. The absence of expression and their drooping eyelids frightened Celia. The looks were similar to her sister's, but these women were strangers to her, and she had no interest in disturbing them. The women in this room looked a bit older, but no less traumatized.

As Celia followed her down the hall, Jane turned into a third, much smaller room, where an older gentleman was speaking to a young woman. The nurse motioned to Celia to stay at the door, while they waited for the man to come to them. He had a cane in his hand and seemed to be having difficulty breathing. Celia noticed his chest rising and falling with every breath. Naturally, she assumed this was Mr. Lattimore. Except for two or three other men who looked like they had been beaten, and were patients of the safehouse, this man in front of her was the only male in the building.

The young woman Lattimore was speaking to was lying in a bed, although this bed did not have a headboard. It was just a mattress on a wooden frame, and it looked out of place in this grand mansion. Next to her were three children: two boys and a little girl, who was the youngest and probably no more than three years old. Although the mother did not look like she would be giving birth soon, she was noticeably pregnant. Celia couldn't understand why this woman was upstairs and not on the main floor with the others. She also wondered why Voula had been taken to another place to give birth. This building was obviously helping women in the same situation. And it was further away from the danger of the fire.

"Why did they not bring Voula to this place?" asked Celia. "It is not as close to the fire, and it is closer to the ships."

"There is no doctor here, at the moment," explained Jane. "And this is not a hospital, my dear. Dr. Preston is at the hospital where Voula was taken, and she will be having her baby very soon. Also, some of the women here are foreigners and have a better chance of leaving the city. Mr. Lattimore thought it would be best for them to be close to the pier."

"Why does that matter?" asked the young girl.

"Well, we could get them on their ships fast, once they have been given the proper paperwork. The ships are instructed to help their own people, no one else," replied the nurse awkwardly, revealing a bit of embarrassment. "The last of the Greek ships have already left and taken their soldiers back home."

"But they will return for us, will they not?" Celia's voice sounded anxious, and she felt abandoned.

"I do not know, my dear," Jane said sheepishly.

While the two were talking, the man was giving the young family some reassurance.

"I will get to the American consulate as soon as possible and inquire about your departure. I am sure you will be able to board one of the ships, without any issues. However, I would advise your husband to stay out of Smyrna, especially if he does not have an American passport. I'll find out what I can and come to see you with any news." He squeezed the woman's hand and patted the shorter boy on the head. He had been holding some papers that he folded and put into his jacket pocket. He turned around and walked towards Celia and the nurse.

As he approached them, Celia noticed a humped back contributing to the unusual gait of his walk. He wore thick glasses with a thin metal frame, but his eyes sparkled with life and spirit. The man's black suit seemed to be much too large for him, as the shoulder seams fell almost an inch too low. Celia could tell he led a humble life; his doubled-up cuffs edged past the sleeves of his sagging suit jacket.

Jonathan Lattimore had fallen in love with Smyrna the moment he arrived with his family. But things had changed drastically, and he had to do the same, quickly. Lilian was not as capable. Watching the refugees as they passed their home had become very frightening for the woman, and she pleaded with Jonathan to return to America. His compassion for the refugees was too great, however. The people in this mansion were the reason he had been brought to the beautiful city, he told her. God sent him to help them, and for now, he was one of their few saviours, until God provided them with a better way. Like most of the Christians in the city, Jonathan believed it was only a matter of time before He would.

He smiled as he came to meet the two women, who were both taller than him. His smile seemed peculiar since his mouth was rather large, and his lips were quite thin. And yet, the man seemed quite cheerful, even though Celia noticed the slight wincing on his face. He had only a few wrinkles on his face, but his illness and exhaustion made him seem much older.

"Hello," he said looking at Celia, and bowing his head slightly, his brown eyes looking over his round pince-nez glasses. "Or rather, Geia sas," he said, before Celia could reply. He assumed the young girl with the brown eyes and curly hair did not speak English.

"Celia, this is Mr. Lattimore. He has been helping the women and children of the city, and the injured, as well. Mr. Lattimore, this is Celia," said Jane, pointing to the young woman.

"Hello," said Celia, and shared a little smile, proud to be showing the man that she did speak some English.

"You speak English?" he asked, leaning into the girl with enthusiasm.

"A little bit," replied the teen. "My brother and I learned it in school and would come to the Quay to listen to the people from other countries."

"Very good. Then, you also speak Greek? Or Armenian?" he asked.

"I speak Greek. I know a little Turkish and even less Armenian," said Celia.

"Mr. Lattimore, I know you mentioned you were looking for someone to go back to the bakeries today. Someone who spoke Greek," said Jane. "Celia can help you. Her mother is somewhere on this Quay, probably close to the French consulate and I am hoping that as you return from the bakeries, she may find her in the crowd."

"Find her in that chaos, Miss DeBlanc?" asked Mr. Lattimore, finding the suggestion absurd and raising his eyebrows. "That is highly unlikely. Where does one begin to look even *close* to the consulate?"

He caught himself quickly, feeling ashamed for being so abrupt and using a harsh tone. He didn't want to embarrass the nurse, nor did he want to discourage the teenage girl. He quickly changed his tone and sounded more spirited.

"But we can worry about that after we try the bakeries and deal with the problem of hunger, first. I don't even know if any of those bakeries are still open. I am hearing that more people have been abandoning their homes and businesses in the Greek and Armenian quarters. The Maltese area is also shutting down, now. But we'll try, won't we, Celia?" he said as he turned to her with a smile. Celia nodded in agreement. She caught herself feeling a bit frustrated because she was supposed to be looking for her family, not helping this man with his problems. But she didn't know how to say no to him, especially because he was helping so many people on the Quay, *her* people.

"Let's go see the children in the other room first, and we can go right away. It's almost 2:00. I hope to be back here by 4:00, my dear," said Mr. Lattimore.

"Yes, sir," replied Celia. As she and Jonathan Lattimore continued to the next room, without a word, Jane proceeded back towards the staircase. Celia felt somewhat abandoned by the nurse, but she knew this man was gentle and kind. Even with his initial small outburst, she felt safe with him.

The fourth room was further down the hall, at the back of the building. As they approached it, Celia could hear the voices of children. There were so many, she couldn't make out any words or languages spoken. When they got to the room, the sun was beaming through the many windows. As much as the light added heat to the room, and made it uncomfortable, Celia found the sunlight a welcome contrast to the dark rooms they had just come from.

There was a large cherry tree outside one of the windows that provided some shade, but for the most part, the room was lit with sunshine. A very large armoire took up one entire wall, and blankets lay on almost the entire floor in this large room. There was no rug on the floor. The only section not covered was close to the armoire where some children were sitting cross-legged. The windows were wide open, and a nice breeze managed to flow through the room.

In the corner next to the windows were two children. One was a boy, maybe eight years old, and the other was a girl, probably four or five. Holding her hand, he stood on his tiptoes trying to see outside the window, and he used his other hand to pull himself up. Celia's eyebrows furrowed in sympathy when she saw the girl had injured her leg; it was bandaged from knee to ankle.

The enormous room measured the size of the first three rooms put together. Unlike the main level, this floor was made of hardwood and the wall opposite the armoire had matching wooden shelves lined with books.

Celia noticed a young woman kneeling, trying to console a little boy who was crying. Her hair was a golden blonde colour, with two delicate pins pulling it to the one side. She didn't look like a nurse or a teacher. And her crisp, modern clothing and clean shoes looked like she hadn't stepped outside but had been parachuted into Smyrna's mayhem from teatime in London.

Celia estimated the room held at least sixty-five young children, and some older girls who were wearing a uniform. From what Celia could see, the young blonde woman cared for all of them.

The uniforms were different from the ones Celia had worn to school. *These girls must be part of a private school, only for girls,* she thought. That was how most private schools were in Smyrna. They were for either boys or girls. Her school was for both, but they were taught in separate parts of the building. The boys were on one side of the school and the girls were on another. Only during recess would the children all meet in the playground.

"Where did they all come from?" Celia asked Mr. Lattimore as they stopped in the doorway.

"Some are orphans, a few of them became separated from their families, and some came from the American Girls' College, here in the city," he explained.

"Are they all American?" she asked.

"No, most are not," he replied. "Only the girls in uniform are American. I found ten of them waiting at a bakery for their teacher to return for them, but she never did. The rest are either Greek or Armenian, we think. Some are too young or too scared to tell us their name. Wait here my dear."

He went to the young woman who had just succeeded in putting a smile on the little boy's face. He was holding a wooden crucifix, and she was holding him in her arms when Mr. Lattimore greeted her. Celia couldn't hear what the little man said to her, but her response was to nod to him, and smile, and then she walked to another group of children who were calling her.

Mr. Lattimore came toward Celia and told her they were ready to leave. She followed him down the stairs, where he told her to wait while he went for his hat. Jonathan returned quickly and the two hurried back onto the street, where the air was slightly fresher.

Chapter 17

A Chance Meeting

"Please stay close to me, my dear. We're going to the consulate first so I can see about Mrs. Kontos' passage. She is the pregnant woman in the small room." Mr. Lattimore walked briskly, considering his slight stature and what Celia believed to be his ill health. He was more than happy to tell her about the woman upstairs as they walked. While the two men were physically different, Mr. Lattimore reminded her of Kyrio Spiro as he spoke to her, trying to be engaging. It was a welcome distraction from the images on the street.

"Her husband is an Armenian diplomat working for the government, but she is American. Her three children were all born here in Smyrna, and we need to get them out. Then, we can continue with our task. Hopefully, we can find someone at the consulate to drive us through the city to the bakeries. We cannot carry all that bread ourselves," said Mr. Lattimore.

The American consulate was on Galazio Street, which was a small side street running southeast off the Quay. As luck would have it, they would have to pass the French consulate on their way. Celia kept close to Mr. Lattimore, but continually looked into the crowds, hoping for a familiar face. She saw no one she knew. And as they approached the spot where she was supposed to reunite with her family, Celia's heart sank. No one. Not even a neighbour or a distant relative's relative. Mr. Lattimore realized Celia had slowed, hoping to find someone in the crowd, but he didn't say a word. He let the girl look, and when they passed the furthest of the two hanging French flags, he could see her put her head down.

"We'll look again on our way back," he said to Celia, and pointed forward with his cane. A sense of relief secretly filled the man, reassured that the young woman would be accompanying him to the bakeries.

They turned left onto Galazio Street and walked up to the consulate with its motionless Stars and Stripes flag hanging at ease. Lattimore and Celia saw a mob of people trying to get inside. The older man took the teen by the hand and pushed his way to the front. *For a small man, he can certainly make people move,* thought Celia, impressed by Mr. Lattimore's tenacity.

"I am an American," he'd say every so often, and people would move for him. As he got to the door, the person holding it shut, a marine dressed in his service uniform, recognized him, and opened it to allow them entry. As the two walked through the door, the marine nodded to both.

The man looked towards Celia and asked Mr. Lattimore who she was.

"She is with me."

"Is she American?"

"No, she is Greek, but we won't be staying long. I am here to speak to someone about getting passage out of the city. The woman in question is with her children and they are staying at the safehouse at 490. She is an American, and her husband, an Armenian, is out of the city at the moment.

"Lucky for him," said the marine, sarcastically. "You can speak to Mr. Herman regarding the required paperwork to get her out of the city, Mr. Lattimore," he said, pointing to a man in a white short-sleeved shirt and grey pants.

Lattimore told the young girl to stand behind the guard and wait for him to return. He walked over to Mr. Herman, and they spoke for a few minutes. The office was bustling with people, both in front of and behind the counters. Most of those behind the counters were removing papers from drawers and throwing them into crates. Others were speaking with people who had come in from the street looking for passports or other paperwork. Celia assumed they were trying to get passage out of the city. Everyone was anxious or angry. One woman at the counter was in tears, pleading for passage for the young companion next to her.

A man was waving his passport at one of the men behind the counter and yelling at him. He kept telling the teller that he was Catalonian and had lived there all his life, except for a few years when he was young and the past eight months, when he had been living in Smyrna. He was now working in this city and the only reason his company had sent him to Smyrna was because he spoke Greek and had been born in Athens. Celia couldn't understand why he would be in an American consulate but realized there was much she probably did not know about the situation. She turned her focus away from the men to Mr. Lattimore.

He dwarfed in comparison to the man Celia assumed was Mr. Herman. Both men looked tired, and it was obvious to Celia that they knew each other. Mr. Lattimore's comfort and familiarity with the people in the office told her this was not the first time he had been in this building.

As Mr. Lattimore was in charge of finding food, he quickly learned that the people on the Quay weren't the only refugees across the city that were hungry. Many Smyrniots had left their homes and congregated in churches, cemeteries, and school courtyards. Most Armenians had fled to Saint Stephanos, while the Greeks had fled to either Saint George or Saint Photini, which was only a few blocks from the YMCA and the consulate.

After their brief discussion, Mr. Lattimore followed Mr. Herman to a desk, where the taller gentleman signed and stamped some papers, then handed them to Mr. Lattimore. Mr. Herman smiled at Mr. Lattimore, nodded, and placed his hand on the smaller man's arm, seeming to offer encouragement and support. Celia heard Mr. Lattimore saying, "Thank you, thank you." He shook Mr. Herman's hand and returned to the young woman.

"Let's go, my dear. The car will be on the corner, waiting for us. We'll have to go back on the Quay and turn down the next street." said Mr. Mr. . He nodded to the marine at the door, who opened it for them while trying to keep the mob outside from entering.

"Please remain here until I call you to come inside!" the marine called to the people outside.

"This way, Celia," Mr. Lattimore said to the young girl as he pointed to the corner further down the street.

Beyond where he was pointing, further south, Celia could see smoke. She couldn't tell where the fire was, but the dark cloud was blowing westward and now hovering over the sea.

They had walked only half-way to the corner when Celia thought she heard someone call her name. Confused, she looked back.

"Celia! Vasilia Alexiou!"

The young woman couldn't find the source of the shouting. She slowed down to look for a familiar face. It was a woman's voice, but whose, she didn't know for certain. As she picked up her pace to catch up to Mr. Lattimore, who hadn't realized she had fallen behind, a hand grabbed her arm. When Celia turned around, she saw her. Kyria Antigone! Celia's eyes popped and she fell into the teacher's arms, elated at seeing her.

"Where are you going, my girl?" shouted the teacher, trying to drown out the noise. "Where is your family?"

By this time, Mr. Lattimore had come back for the teenager.

"Do you know this woman, Celia?" he asked. Celia finally let go of Kyria Antigone and turned to Mr. Lattimore with delight and excitement.

"Yes, this is Kyria Antigone. She is the teacher I told you about," said Celia, "the one who began to teach us English." She turned to the woman and in her more comfortable Greek language, said "My mother and sisters are somewhere here on the Quay, I think. I just do not know where they are right now."

Realizing Kyria Antigone didn't have both her arms around her during their embrace, Celia looked down. Next to the teacher stood a little girl, her daughter. She looked to be two or three years old and was hiding behind her mother's skirt as she held her hand. Noticing Celia was watching her, the bashful little girl grabbed her mother's skirt hem and wrapped it around her little body. She spun herself around a couple times before Antigone picked her up to make sure she stayed close to her. She looked at Celia and she smiled intensely. It was refreshing to see a smiling child. This little girl was obviously too young to understand what was going on around her, which was probably for the best.

"Where are you going with this man?" asked Antigone. The woman spoke English purposely, to make the little man subtly aware that she was suspicious of him.

"Kyria, my name is Jonathan Lattimore. I am the co-director of the YMCA and I'm with the relief effort. Celia is coming with me to get more bread for the refugees here on the Quay and other areas, too. They are coming continuously from the interior. I need someone who can speak Greek because most of the bakeries I am familiar with are owned by Greek families. And they are the ones most willing to help," said the gentleman.

"Is this true, Celia?" asked the teacher.

"Yes, Kyria. As soon as I am finished helping Mr. Lattimore, I will look for my mother and sisters."

"How will you find them, Celia? This is a madhouse. Do you know where they are? You cannot look for them alone."

Mr. Lattimore interjected, trying to ease the teacher's concerns. "Kyria Antigone, we will be travelling with an American Marine escort, in a car. And, as soon as we return from the bakeries, I will help Celia find her family, you have my word. If we don't find them, I will keep her inside the safehouse with the other women and nurses. I think she will be better off in there, than out here. Be sure that God will watch over her and the rest of us."

Celia saw Mr. Lattimore lower his head slightly without losing eye contact with the woman. He gave the teacher a look that not only satisfied Kyria Antigone but gave her relief. Mr. Lattimore was Christian and an American, and this gave the teacher a sense of security. Kyria Antigone nodded and faintly smiled.

"Alright, Celia. Be very careful, and DO NOT GO ANYWHERE ALONE!" As she said this to the young girl, she held her hand firmly and looked straight into her eyes. "Do you hear me? And when you get back and into this mob, stay in the centre as much as possible. Do not stay close to the side roads." Tears welled up in the young teacher's eyes. "I don't know how, but we will find our way out of here. God is high above."

"Yes, Kyria Antigone, I understand." The young girl hugged her teacher goodbye.

Celia couldn't understand what the teacher meant about staying away from the side roads, but didn't bother to ask about it.

"I need to go back to my spot before someone takes our mat. My sister is with me and my children, and I told her to watch my son for me. But she can only do so much, alone with three children of her own." The woman lowered her head, and her words shrivelled into a whisper. It was the first time Celia heard sorrow in the teacher's voice. But she checked herself immediately.

"If I see your mother, I will tell her I have seen you. She will be relieved, I know. May the Holy Mother be with you, my girl," said the teacher, as she tightened her grip on the young girl's hand for the last time.

"And with you, Kyria," replied Celia as she began to walk away, waving at the little girl.

"Geia sas," called out the little one, and Celia flashed a big smile back to her.

Mr. Lattimore took Celia by the elbow, and they continued along the street, leading to the next side road. It was so nice to have seen someone familiar, thought Celia. It gave her a much-needed sense of hope. *Finally, someone I know.*

Chapter 18

Home No Longer

As Celia walked with the American she remained quiet, but her mind was not at rest. Thinking about her mother and sisters, looking for more familiar faces, and bumping into people along the street, Celia felt caught in a funnel. She knew enough to stay close to Mr. Lattimore and allow him to lead the way. He pointed to where they were going to turn, and while Celia noticed the smoke in the far south, she was too distracted to become affected by it. They turned the corner onto Galazio Street, expecting to see a car, but there was no vehicle in sight. She saw that Mr. Lattimore didn't seem concerned that the street was eerily quiet.

"We may have to wait a few minutes, my dear," said Lattimore, trying to catch his breath from the walk. "Let's go across the street where the sun is not hitting us, directly."

He stopped in the middle of the road began to cough incessantly, and Celia became concerned.

"Are you okay, Mr. Lattimore?"

"Yes, yes, my dear," he replied, beginning to calm down. "I had tuberculosis when I was a young man."

"Oh," said Celia nervously, not knowing what the disease was.

"Oh, please do not be afraid, I'm not contagious. I would never subject anyone to this disease if I were," he told the young woman, trying to put her at ease. "I just don't have the same lung capacity, as I used to. Almost half of us never do, and we struggle with shortness of breath," he explained.

"I'm sorry to hear that," she said with concern. He nodded, and pointed to the other side of the road, continuing to cross.

Celia followed and they waited next to a closed gate. As she leaned on it, Celia found its warmth reminded her of the others she had come across that day, and it sent her mind racing, again. *Did Voula make it to the hospital? Where was Anastasia, now? Is she strong enough to keep walking?* she wondered. Celia looked back toward the Quay and saw the dismal mob of people struggling to find a direction. Many were looking aimlessly around their immediate area; others had buried their faces in their hands. A few were sitting, rocking back and forth. From Celia's point of view, it wasn't possible to tell if they were trying to calm a small child, or just themselves.

She looked in the opposite direction, into the city's core and noticed something strange in the street. While some of the homes in this area had not yet been broken into or set on fire, one on the corner had signs of a forced entry. The door was wide open and some of the glass windows had been broken. Household items had also been strewn across the front of the home, and it was obvious a fire had been started inside. There was some lingering smoke, but Celia supposed someone must have put it out before it could spread to the building next to it. The open door and broken windows didn't reveal anything but darkness inside the building, and silence. Celia guessed it was an office of a professional. A lawyer or architect, perhaps.

As if out of a complex dream, she saw two rats in front of the door. They were large, almost black. And although they looked like typical rats, there was something odd about them: they were running after one another in a circle,. They were so close to one another that the tail of one was almost in the mouth of the other. They were not going anywhere else, only running away from each other, staying in the same two-foot area. They made no sound, other than the slapping of their ugly feet as they scurried through the dirt. No squealing, nothing. They ran as though trapped in their own madness and ignorant of any other presence. Mr. Lattimore, who was finally breathing comfortably, looked at Celia and followed her eyes, noticing the same image.

"When they sense trouble, the rats run outside to safety, just as people do," he said.

"But they're not going anywhere. They're just running after each other. Rats frighten me," said Celia, squinting, and turning up her nose in revulsion.

"Don't be frightened, my girl," said Mr. Lattimore. "We are all God's creatures. During the French Revolution, people relied on those animals for sustenance. As horrible as it sounds, and may it never get to that point, here, God has a plan for us all."

"Why do they keep running in the same circle?" Celia asked, ignoring Mr. Lattimore's comment about God.

"Maybe they just don't want to go anywhere else, my dear. They just may like where they are," said Mr. Lattimore. As disgusted as Celia was at the sight of rats, Mr. Lattimore's explanation was enough to almost generate sympathy for the creatures. She sighed and looked at him as he faintly smiled at her, lifting his eyebrows. He is right. They are all God's creatures, she thought to herself.

The same black Chevrolet with the American flag that had taken Voula to the Dutch hospital appeared from beyond the rats. As it approached, the rodents disappeared under a large chair which had been thrown in front of the building. The car came to a halt in front of its next passengers and Mr. Lattimore opened the door for Celia. It was the first time she had ever ridden in a car. She had sat in one last year, but this was the first time she had gone anywhere as a passenger. This car also had windows and a solid upper frame, unlike those she had seen before which had had no top at all.

The driver and Mr. Lattimore exchanged greetings, and the older gentleman introduced the young woman to the driver. His name was Mr. Briggs, and he wore a uniform different from the man in the consulate. Celia didn't recognize what type it was but guessed he was in the American navy. She also realized he wasn't the same driver who had taken Kyria Eleni and Voula to the hospital. Although she hadn't been able to get a good look at the other man, Mr. Briggs' light blond hair and his height made him very recognizable, and she guessed he was most likely in his thirties. He towered over Mr. Lattimore and, although he didn't pay much attention to Celia, was polite enough.

Celia sat in the back seat with Mr. Lattimore. She was directly behind the driver and could see his hazel eyes in the rear-view mirror. While she was familiar with mirrors, of course, the car's mirror caught her attention, a most innocent of distractions in a time of chaos. Mesmerized by it, she tilted her head only slightly, making various images appear and disappear from sight. Celia constantly turned her head behind her to check on what had recently dropped out of view. It was only when she noticed the driver watching her in the mirror and heard him quietly chuckling, she stopped moving about in the car and sat quietly in her seat.

"Do you know where we are going, Mr. Briggs?" asked Lattimore as the car jolted into gear.

"Yes, Mr. Lattimore," replied the driver. "Mr. Herman told me we are to go to the same bakeries we went to a few days ago. But, Mr. Lattimore, I must tell you that I have driven by some of those since yesterday, and most are either abandoned or closed. The ones closer to the Armenian quarters are gone. Burned, sir. But we can go and see what options we have, Mr. Lattimore."

"Yes, Mr. Briggs, I have seen them, too. Let's try to get as much as we can. There are only going to be more people coming to the city," replied the older man. "Try the furthest ones first, and we can walk to the ones closest to the Quay if we have to."

Briggs agreed and continued driving. Celia had been startled by the powerful roar of the Chevrolet vehicle, but became quickly at ease.

They drove past the same streets Celia had passed earlier that morning. It was a peculiar feeling to be in a car. Celia could feel most of the bumps in the road and wondered how Voula had endured them. Briggs also had to be careful to try to avoid the rubble and the bodies that lay in the streets. He also made the effort to drive past the victims rather quickly so there wouldn't be too much time to look at them.

Celia soon realized that she preferred to look up at the buildings and the sky. It was the only place her eyes could rest without being reminded of the horrors in her city. The car windows were down and the blowing air, although still smoke-ridden, was better than the foul smells she had left behind on the Quay. For a few brief seconds, Celia closed her eyes and hoped her next breath of air would be fresh, or maybe smell of pastries, or flowers. But her lungs absorbed only a deep breath of smoke that choked her and brought on a quick cough.

The driver slowed down in front of the first bakery that had, in fact, been broken into. From the street, they could see the bodies of two people inside. Blood was visible on the door's remaining glass, and on the floor, and it flowed into the street. There was no bread to be seen on the shelves. It had either been taken already, or it had never been made. Celia saw Mr. Lattimore slowly shake his head with sorrow. Without a word, the driver continued to the next bakery, which was only a few minutes away. As they slowed and approached it, Celia gasped. The windows had been broken and soldiers were standing inside, smoking their cigarettes. This was the closest she had been to any soldiers since they had taken her father and brother away. There were no victims to be seen, but the condition of the building told her it would be best to leave immediately. Celia was relieved that Mr. Briggs and Mr. Lattimore had the same reservations as she did.

Mr. Briggs continued to the next bakery. As he approached an intersection, he stopped the car and turned his head back to motion to Mr. Lattimore. Ahead of them, an entire building was engulfed in a fire. Celia had never seen such a blaze and could feel the heat that was fanning out from the three-storey property which lay roughly a hundred feet ahead. The grace of the pyre's movement was mesmerizing until something within the building came to a crashing burst of embers, exploding through the windows and broken door.

A small crowd ran from the building next to the fire, holding bags and mats. Their faces seemed dirty, and they looked around, aimlessly. A man from the group pointed towards a building across the narrow street as though instructing the others where to go.

Suddenly, they heard a gunshot, which startled Celia and the two men in the car. They could hear some of the people ahead scream, but they instantly stopped, then began to scurry around, still trying to find a place to hide. Celia and the men wondered where the shot had come from, since there were no signs of soldiers in the area. She looked everywhere she could from her seat, and still saw nothing. A man fell to the ground with a thud and the bundle he was carrying emptied out onto the dirt road. While Celia and the men continued to look at the crowd on the run, they noticed none of them slowed down to help their fellow escapee or pick up his belongings.

"Up there." Briggs pointed to the top of a building. As Lattimore and Celia leaned forward to look, they noticed a sniper had been on the roof of a three-storey building, likely waiting for people to exit their hiding places. He wore a fez and a soldier's uniform, and he was waving to someone. Across from him, atop another roof, a second armed soldier was calling out to him in delight. Waiting for their prey to appear from the buildings was a game to these men. Listening to their laughs initially confused Celia. She did not understand what was happening nor how gruesome these men were until she heard Mr. Briggs bitterly say the word "animals" under his breath.

Celia didn't know if she should feel relieved that someone else was as disgusted by the soldiers as she was or scared that there weren't enough people to do something about them. But Celia was sure about one thing: she was angry and had started to understand how so many people in the city hated Turks.

"Mr. Lattimore, we're close to the Armenian part of the city. I know there are three bakeries in that direction. But I would advise that we do not attempt to go that way," said Briggs, pointing ahead.

"I agree. We will have to try the others," said Lattimore, deflated.

Briggs turned left, and Celia looked at his eyes in the mirror in front of her. His head bobbed from side to side, looking from the rear-view mirror on the outside of his door to the rear-view mirror inside the car. From one side of the street to the other. Bodies lay on the sides of the road, and he was careful to avoid them. Every so often, the driver would shake his head in frustration, and Celia noticed he was beginning to get angry. He huffed as they drove by two men beating a man with a stick as they pulled him out of a building . Under his breath he cursed them with a word Celia couldn't understand. It was then that Briggs caught the young girl looking at him in the rear-view mirror and he checked himself. But he continued to keep looking in all directions. Both Celia and Jonathan remained quiet in the back seat.

One by one, they drove past three other bakeries; all of them had either been abandoned, broken into, or was in flames . The homes along the route were mostly open, their doors either broken or left ajar, with much of their contents thrown in the streets. It was now past 2:00, and the smell was almost as bad as it had been on the Quay, the smoke choking, and the fire not only visible but growing. Loud explosions could often be heard from various areas of the city as roofs crashed to the ground. Celia could hear Mr. Lattimore huffing in irritation. She knew some people from the Armenian quarter and wondered where they were now. Probably on the waterfront, with her own family, she thought. Many had run to churches, to schools, even cemeteries.

They passed the American Collegiate Institute for Girls, where the girls from the safehouse had come from. After three or four kilometres, the car came to a halt. Celia couldn't understand why Mr. Briggs had stopped. She looked around, but could not see anything unusual through the side windows. Lattimore pulled himself forward trying to understand what was happening. Before he could ask, Briggs broke the silence.

"What are they doing?" he asked. He was squinting, and slowly shaking his head from side to side.

Celia glanced at him to see he was looking straight ahead. She leaned slightly towards Mr. Lattimore so she could look through the vehicle's front window, and she saw a band of troops. unloading barrels from a truck. As she focused further down the street, past the soldiers, she could see they had unloaded some barrels already, which they seemed to have placed strategically an equal distance apart from each other. Further back, behind the barrels, was a cloud of smoke so large that Mount Pagos was barely visible. Celia squinted, desperately looking for the outline of its ancient citadel, but it was as if someone had picked it up off the hill and walked away with it.

Chapter 19
An Old City Changes

The mountain was home to the grand Kadifekale Castle, built in the third century BC. Most days, the structure looked like a crown, set upon the peak. The original location of Smyrna had at one time been further north, at the base of Mount Yamanlar, and it was later moved to the base of Pagos, stretching to the harbour, where it stood now. Celia remembered hearing the story about two goddesses visiting Alexander the Great, who was asleep under a tree; they told him to move the city closer to the sea. And she'd heard how the Romans created cisterns that were the centre of the city's drinking water network. The Byzantines and Ottomans had renovated them, and their remains were still visible in Smyrna's ancient agora. She knew the city was famous, historically and biblically.

As one poet had said, Smyrna was like "the mother goddess Cybele with her feet on the sea and her head crowned with a circle of beautiful buildings." It was thought there had been a statue of the Mother Goddess on the slope of Pagos to the east. Celia knew all this from her teachers, her parents, and her priests, but her eyes were telling her they had all been wrong. There was nothing beautiful in front of her now, and the only hope that the Christian God could offer was floating up to the heavens, caught in the smoke that was suffocating the city.

In Revelations 2:10, John of Patmos tells the Church of Smyrna "Fear none of those things which thou shalt suffer: behold, the devil shall cast some of you into prison, that ye may be tried; and ye shall have tribulation ten days: be thou faithful unto death, and I will give thee a crown of life." This "crown of life" was believed to be the peak of Pagos. Many of the Christians of Smyrna would hear these words over the recent years as the priests of the city would try to calm their fears. During festivals, people would make crowns of yellow spurge to symbolize the impending immortality their God had promised them. Visitors to the city would be welcomed with these wreaths, along with wishes for a happy and eternal life. The Christians had remained faithful to the words of John.

As Celia remembered all she had learned at school and in church, terror told her they were just words. The soldiers didn't care about Cybele and Alexander. And God's promise of immortality was a lie. What the priest had said was a lie. What her parents had said about the kindness of all people was a lie. *There's no God to save us from this*, she told herself.

But those on the Quay felt differently. Their belief in deliverance from the oncoming enemy was steadfast. While autumn brought the last of the fruit, hope lingered within reach. However, few of them had seen what Celia had. Only those marching towards the east into the desert were beginning to feel as Celia did. And once their beaten and exhausted bodies fell to the dirt, no one would hear their last confession, no one would give them their last Holy Communion from a golden chalice and spoon. They would not be bathed in oil, nor have two coins placed over their eyes to prepare them for their journey down the river Styx to face Charon. Cerberus would not be guarding them. Only the dogs and vultures of *this* world would find them.

"I think it's best we turn around, Mr. Briggs," said Lattimore, calmly. He hadn't finished his words before the driver had begun shifting the car into reverse. As he did so, one of the soldiers looked up and saw the car. He shouted to one of his comrades, pointing to the Chevy. Celia saw the second man motion to him that it was nothing to be concerned with. His gesture told the lower-ranking soldier that the car had an American flag on it. While the two soldiers were discussing the onlookers, one of the others placed a pump in the barrel he was tending and began to spray the building with its contents. All three in the car swallowed their angst, and their eyes widened at the scene in front of them. Celia felt as though her heart was about to burst from her chest, and her body exploded with a sense of heat greater than what she had already been experiencing only a few moments earlier.

"I think it's also a good idea to have the young lady try to hide from their view, Mr. Lattimore," said Briggs, who was looking back, still driving in reverse, trying to find a place to turn around. There was already rubble in the street, and as annoying as it was to drive through it normally, driving in reverse was even more of a challenge.

Lattimore motioned Celia to sit on the floor of the car, to avoid the attention of the soldiers. Celia immediately obeyed, falling to the floor, trembling like a leaf about to leave its branch in a brisk wind. While the American flag could help the car's occupants, they were outnumbered and if they were stopped, a young Greek girl could be a problem.

It did not take Briggs a long time to find a place to turn the car around but, before doing so, the group in the car realized what was in the barrels. The smell of gasoline permeated the air, so much that Lattimore closed the rear windows. As Celia looked up from her seat on the floor, she could see that Briggs kept looking in the mirror to make sure they weren't being followed. It became clear to her that she was a liability to the people who were trying to help the refugees. Tears filled her eyes, and she quickly buried her face in her knees so no one would see her face. *Calming an emotional girl was the last thing these men needed to be doing,* she thought to herself. Shame and guilt are horrible burdens to be carried by someone not even fifteen years old.

Once they turned onto another street, Mr. Lattimore told Celia she could sit back up on the seat. She was relieved to hear the words, realizing she did not like the feeling of not knowing where she was. Claustrophobia was setting in, and she noticed her breathing had become heavier. The motion of the car had also made her a bit nauseous while she sat on the floor. Celia quickly jumped into her seat and immediately recognized the street they were on. They were back in the Greek district of the city and would be passing her school within the next kilometre. She had walked this route every day with Maria and was half-expecting to be doing so again, within the next week. Celia forgot for a minute that she had graduated and was supposed to be attending a private teachers' school in just a few weeks. So much had changed that day that becoming a teacher was already becoming just a dream.

As they drove past the school Celia saw the building had been vandalized, its doors and windows broken and smoke coming through one of the classrooms that had once been hers. She quietly stared at the school for as long as the ride would allow. A large pile of debris lay at the edge of the school's property. "STOP!" cried Lattimore, suddenly. Briggs brought the Chevy to a screeching halt, sending dust into the air and Celia into the back of Briggs' seat.

"What is it, Mr. Lattimore?" asked Briggs. "Miss, are you okay?" Celia looked into the mirror to catch Briggs' eyes and nodded.

"Over there," shouted Mr. Lattimore. "That girl sitting on a pile of rubble. Celia, stay in the car with Mr. Briggs, I'll go get her," he said.

He got out of the car and carefully walked to the girl. It was difficult to maneuver in the debris, especially for this small man whose health limited his mobility. Celia watched him as he carefully walked up to the girl, and he saw him call out to her as he approached. But the girl was motionless, her head looking down into her lap. Celia wondered if the girl had been separated from her family and was crying. The size of her body told the teenager she was much younger than she was, maybe even younger than Maria. Her dishevelled dark hair did not reach past her shoulders, and her head was tilted to the one side; she was probably feeling lost, Celia thought. She was concerned the girl might be afraid of Mr. Lattimore, and not realize he was there to help. The child would not know he would be offering to take her to the safehouse on the Quay. The girl didn't even turn to look at him, however. *It's unusual that she's not even looking up at him or talking to him. Of course! She doesn't speak English*, thought Celia. She wondered if she should go help talk her into coming with them. It also occurred to Celia that she might know the girl, given they were so close to her own home.

Before she could open the car door, she saw the little man instantly put his hand to his mouth, step back, and fall amongst the rubble. Celia gasped at seeing Mr. Lattimore fall, wondering if he had hurt himself. She didn't understand why the girl would have scared him so much. *What did she say to him?* Even Briggs became concerned for the man, and immediately jumped out of the car.

"Stay here!" he shouted to Celia.

As he had done many times already in Smyrna, Jonathan Lattimore thought he was approaching an innocent little girl. His experiences with children were always positive because they always trusted him ... his voice, his demeanour. And being a smaller man, he was not imposing. Children usually felt safe with him. But he had never seen the evil of humanity staring back at him from a child, until now. As he lay on the ground, Jonathan felt the crushing of a thousand buildings on his chest. The dead child had a piece of wood stuck into her from behind, coming up through her mouth. Her assailants had positioned her in such a way that she looked as if she was sitting, waiting for help. Lattimore had never witnessed such an atrocity against a human being, let alone a child, and couldn't fathom that man could be so depraved. No such beast could be created or even imagined. Where could it come from?

Jonathan became nauseous as he struggled to get up, trying to find his hat and cane. Although he still wore his glasses, he couldn't see. His tears came from the pain of the child's predicament and the gagging within his frail body. From afar, he saw Briggs' silhouette pop out from the car, about to come to his aid, but he waved at him, gesturing to him to get back inside the vehicle. Confused, the driver complied.

After finding his cane, Jonathan walked as fast as he could to the car, and would have fallen again, had he not been as close to it as he was, and able to find somewhere to lean. Opening the door, he staggered onto the front seat, heaving to find a breath. Both Briggs and Celia were in shock, each asking him if he was okay.

"Go, go," he said to Briggs, who had his hand on the struggling man's back. The driver bent over to help him and asked him what happened, but Lattimore just repeated his command to leave, waving his arm for Briggs to drive rather than help him. The car door was barely closed when the Chevy's wheels squealed and threw a cluster of dirt into the air.

"What about the girl?" asked Celia from the back seat, leaning forward to see Mr. Lattimore. She was stunned that they were leaving so abruptly and without the child. "Are we not going to help her?"

H took a few moments to calm himself, trying to take in as much air as possible. "Thankfully, that young woman is with God now. She is in a far better place, my dear," said Lattimore, with difficulty, as he propped himself higher in the seat. Celia couldn't see the tears streaming down the man's cheeks. She could hear him sniffling and see him shaking his head into the palms of his hands. Mr. Briggs' eyes widened, and his jaw dropped as he watched Jonathan weep. Celia could see the driver's chest rise and fall quickly, as he struggled with what to do or say. She desperately wanted to know what had happened but realized it would be better to be quiet. She understood that the girl was dead.

As they drove, no one spoke. Lattimore leaned his head on the window of the passenger side. All the windows were slightly opened to allow for airflow, but the smoke was so intense in this part of the city, it was best to close them again. On two occasions, Briggs drove down a street, only to have to turn around due to the rubble blocking the roadway, or a group of people who, seemed to be ready to attack at any moment.

Not all of them were soldiers. In fact, most were civilian men and even young boys celebrating the new regime. The car may have been American, but Briggs didn't want to risk any confrontations with them. These men held sticks and carried pictures of a man wearing a fez, yelling words no one in the car could hear. Celia would hold her breath every time they came close to soldiers or men she thought were Turkish.

She was grateful to have Mr. Briggs in the car, who seemed to be very conscious of her presence. *Not one loaf of bread, yet. All this driving and risk and not one loaf,* she brooded.

On one street, a mob of people was dragging a barefoot man by his arms. The building behind them was overwhelmed by thick smoke, where no flames were even visible. The attackers stood the man up and began to empty his pockets while beating him at the same time. They then began removing his clothes, but Briggs again, turned the car around, and no one in the car knew what happened to him.

The driver took them to a small narrow street on the outskirts of the Greek Quarter, and not far from the Quay. They had driven almost full circle. By the time they arrived at the next bakery, Lattimore had composed himself and even smiled when they approached their destination. And for good reason.

Finally! This bakery was open and had not been vandalized. Inside, there was nothing on the shelves, no one standing behind the counter. But it was clean, and full of sunlight. It was as if this hidden little store knew nothing of what was happening in the rest of Smyrna.

"Come Celia. These people do not speak a word of English. I met them two days ago and I had my interpreter tell them that I would return for more bread. I do hope they have it," said Mr. Lattimore. They walked into the bakery, but no one could be seen. "Kyrie Stelio!" he called out.

At last! thought Celia. A pleasing scent… freshly baked bread! It was the sweetest smell she had sensed all day, and couldn't get enough of it, as she took deep breaths. She hadn't realized how hungry she had been. The last thing she had eaten was some cheese and bread earlier that morning with her mother and sisters. She remembered the pomegranates on the kitchen floor that Maria had picked up and put in the bag they had taken with them to the pier. How she wished she could have some fruit, now. Or even better, some of the bread she was smelling.

From a back room, a man came out slowly, looking carefully to see who was calling his name. He was a very tall, stout man with a dark moustache and brown eyes. He was mostly bald, but what was left of his hair had small curls in it. Had she met him on the street, Celia would be intimidated by this Kyrie Stelio. He wore a white apron that looked like it had just been washed and pressed. It was spotless and seemed to have been made specifically for his large frame. His face had a scratch on it, just above the left side of his jaw. It wasn't long or even deep, but when he came out in full view, Celia and Mr. Lattimore noticed his hand was also injured and wrapped. It seemed a bit swollen, but it also didn't look to be something he was too concerned about. He realized his injuries had been noticed and smiled at his two customers, revealing a missing tooth.

"Tous katafera," he said, proudly, while raising his injured hand.

Mr. Lattimore turned to Celia and asked her what the man said.

"He said he beat them," she said, smiling slightly.

"I hope they don't come back, Kyrie Stelio," said Mr. Lattimore, although he knew they would, and likely with help.

Celia told the Greek man what the American had said, and Stelio nodded in agreement.

"Yes, they will. I will be closed and gone when they do. I have been waiting for Mr. Jonathan to take the bread. My wife heard that the other bakeries are closed, so we used all the flour we had. I didn't want to leave until you came.

"Wait," said the baker to Celia. He went to the back, while Celia interpreted his words to Mr. Lattimore. He returned with four bags, two in each hand, with six loaves of bread in each bag. He placed them on the counter and with Jonathan and Celia's help they repeated this seven times. Each time she came out from the kitchen, Celia was relieved to see Mr. Briggs was still parked in front. Soon enough, there were almost 170 loaves of bread sitting on the counter. Lattimore turned around to signal the driver, asking for an extra set of hands.

"Please start taking these bags to the car, Celia," said Mr. Lattimore. "I'll pay Kyrie Stelio and be right there."

He pulled a large amount of money out of his pocket, more than Celia had ever seen. The Greek man thanked him, picked up some of the bags and proceeded to help take them to the front door. There was no more room in the car to pick up any other bread from the remaining bakeries, even if they were open. They had to hold some of the bags in their arms because there wasn't any more room on the seats or the floor. As they situated themselves in the car, Celia saw the Greek baker lock the door behind them, remove his apron, and run to the back.

The sweet smell of fresh bread infused the Chevy so much that it made Celia dizzy with delight. It was pleasing to everyone in the car, and Celia was happy to take it back to the Quay. The loaves were stacked so that she couldn't see outside the window to her left. And while Angela had always scolded the children for dropping bread on the ground, even the slightest piece small enough for a bird, in order to fit all of the food in the car, some sat on the floor of the car. *This was God's gift to us, Jesus' body in Holy Communion.* Celia was grateful on behalf of her people.

Mr. Briggs began to drive off and before they could get to the end of the block, Celia noticed four men walking towards the direction they had just come from. One wore a fez and carried a rifle, while the other three held pieces of wood. Of the three men holding sticks, one had a swollen face that had probably come into contact with Kyrie Stelio's fist. She quietly prayed for the man.

"Heavens, that bread smells good," said the driver. Lattimore looked at both the girl and the driver, smiled, and pulled one loaf out of the on his lap. He broke it in half, and ripped pieces for Celia, himself, and Mr. Briggs. No one spoke until they arrived at their destination, being too busy eating. Briggs drove straight to the American consulate.

Chapter 20

That Which We Cannot Control

As they turned onto the Quay, it was clear to Celia that the mob of people had grown. They were now congregating in the side streets, as well as at the waterfront. And yet they seemed quieter than they had been earlier in the day. Exhaustion, heat, and despair had taken the motivational fuel that had previously keeping them motivated and determined. The sun was now directly over the Quay, where the buildings could no longer provide any shade. Many people were sitting or lying on the ground, the lucky ones on mats. Occasionally, a braying lamb or a crying child could be heard, but for the most part, the Quay's noise level had been reduced to a quiet rumbling.

Had it still been summer, at this time of day, people would be home for their afternoon naps. Celia knew that by three or four o'clock it would be normal for the city to have been quiet and the Quay to be empty. Later in the early evening, people would start returning and enjoying the breeze coming off the sea, her family included. She and Mihali could often be found sitting with their father, watching, and listening to people on the Quay, and seeing the familiar faces of friends and family members . At times, Simo would find some of his colleagues or friends and discuss politics or business, while Celia and her brother would try to sit closer to Anglophones at the Café or Sporting Club. If any of their friends were nearby, the two siblings would go their separate ways. If Maria hadn't found any of her own friends to play with, she'd be running between the members of her family.

Celia would sometimes join Angela and Anastasia, who would be browsing the windows of the shops or gazing at the many female tourists who walked along the Quay like it were a Parisian catwalk. Angela would pick out the more fashionable outfits, and test Anesta on how she would replicate it, and with what fabrics. The young woman had become quite competent at recreating clothing designs and was hoping to begin sewing on her own.

But Celia knew she couldn't turn back time. Looking at all the people on the Quay, it was difficult to imagine that her family had been together on the Quay only a few weeks ago. She even remembered Simo telling her and Mihali how he looked forward to Christmas because it was so hot that day.

By now, children would normally be telling their parents about their first days at school. They would be listing off their new friends and talking about their new teacher. Farmers would be exhausted from their day at work, harvesting the crops that were now in season. So many fruits, so many spices. Normally, the city would be full of the aroma of grapes, peaches, figs, and watermelons, not human sewage, sweat, and blood. Celia knew that most of the people here today knew that would not be returning to their homes. They would have to leave, but they were no longer asking themselves where they were going, but rather who would be taking them, and how soon.

On the Quay, Briggs drove very slowly. Once again, Celia was desperate to find a familiar face in the mob. Since many people were now sitting on blankets and rugs on the ground, the sea was more visible, as were the many ships in the harbour. Celia was able to count twenty-two of them Only a few of them were close to the pier and, for the most part, they were still motionless, still quiet. She could see approximately ten whaleboats coming and going to the larger ships, like she had seen earlier in the day. Now, there were more people in them, but they did not appear to be refugees.

Briggs slowly approached the consulate, where four American sailors now stood, guarding its entrance. As he drove, the few lethargic people there moved out of his way. Some even had faint smiles on their faces, trying to be respectful of what the car and, more particularly, the flag, represented.

The car came to a stop. Briggs got out and made his way through the small crowd that was willing to battle the scorching heat, waiting in line to gain entrance to the consulate. He told his passengers to wait while he found out what to do with the bread. Celia continued to look out the window into the crowd, hoping to see her family or even Kyria Antigone. For a quick second, she thought she saw the old man who had told her about the safehouse earlier that morning. Even *he* would be a welcome sight, simply because he was from her neighbourhood. But the man disappeared from her sight. Mr. Lattimore opened the door and got out, just as Briggs was returning to the car.

"Mr. Lattimore, some sailors will be coming out shortly to take the bread. They will be able to distribute it to the crowd. We don't want a commotion, so we'll wait for them."

"Very good," said Lattimore as he turned to Celia. Speaking to her through her open window he said, "Once they take it, Celia, we can begin to look for your mother. If we don't find your family tonight, don't be afraid. You can stay at the safehouse, and we can look again tomorrow." Celia nodded and smiled in appreciation. As horrible as the smell on the Quay was, and as miserable as everyone looked, Celia was much more content being close to the pier than in the city's core. She felt closer to her family and, thankfully, there was no sign of soldiers. She also felt relieved that she was able to help Mr. Lattimore. It was unfortunate that only one bakery was open, but even the little help she had given made her feel proud. She even felt like more of an adult, especially being in the midst of such people

Four men dressed in white came to the car, and before they opened its doors, they looked around, making sure they could take the loaves of bread inside without being overrun by the crowd. One sailor was quite young, no more than nineteen. He caught the teen girl's attention from the moment he walked out the door. He had short, light brown hair and brown eyes. His lips were full, and his jaw square. As he walked toward the car, he acknowledged the presence of the refugees that were close by, graciously waiting for them to pass. She saw him look at her, as well, and he faintly smiled. They were still looking at each other when he reached into the car and grabbed the bread that was sitting on Celia's lap. He didn't notice that as he reached for the loaves of bread, his hand went under her skirt, instead of above it. The grazing of his hand on her knee, made Celia jump, startling the young man who hit his head on the car roof.

"I'm so sorry, Miss," he said, and his face immediately turned red. "I didn't mean to touch ... I mean ... I … I was told to come and quickly get the bags in the car. My apologies."

"I'm well. You hugged me, sir," said Celia incorrectly, blushing from embarrassment. Her hands immediately went into her lap, and she turned her head away from him. She realized her choice of words was wrong and she gasped in shame. A feeling of nausea came over her, as she firmly rubbed her thighs, trying to erase what had just happened.

Hearing her say "hugged" confused the young man, and realizing the young girl may have used the wrong word to express herself, he quickly picked up five of the bags of bread and darted back into the building. The five-second ordeal caught the attention of Mr. Lattimore, who immediately responded.

"Is something wrong, Celia? Did that young man do something to you?" he asked.

"No, no," replied the young girl. "He did not do any wrong. I say the wrong word at him," she said, still fumbling with her English words. Her face becoming red as a beet; Celia was overwhelmed by what was happening. There was a humanitarian crisis unfolding around her and, for the first time in her life, she was proud that she was contributing to help the thousands of people who sat within less than a mile's radius of her. But a primeval part of herself had been exposed, and she could not control herself.

Mr. Lattimore looked baffled and as Mr. Herman had just come to greet the man, he, too, noticed Celia's flustered demeanour.

"Is the young lady not feeling well, Mr. Lattimore?" he asked his friend. Lattimore told him that everything was fine, realizing that what may have just happened was innocent adolescent awkwardness.

"Oh," replied Herman, a bit confused. The girl was looking away from him, towards the harbour. She quickly turned again, looking at Mr. Lattimore.

"Can we start looking for my mother now?" she blurted. Tears of shame had almost formed in her eyes, and she wanted to change the subject. She had never been so mortified and did not know what more to say to stop the inquiries and the stares.

"Are you sure you're okay, Miss?" asked the head of the consulate.

"Yes, yes, I am very good," she said, trying to sound as if nothing had just happened.

"She is fine, Mr. Herman," said Lattimore. "She has had a very long day. It's been a long day for everyone today, especially for young people."

"Indeed," replied Herman, who seemed relieved there was not yet another issue he had to deal with. He stood in front of the car door for a moment, looking at Lattimore with concern.

"Jonathan, I'm glad you're here. I have formally ordered the evacuation of all Americans in the city. Reports are saying that the fires are out of control now. Please see to it that your family will be at the American theatre by five o'clock. Spread the word to others in Paradise." Herman sounded concerned and was very explicit about getting people out of Smyrna.

He and his wife had already sent their daughter to Greece at the beginning of the month, but he had many more Americans to reach throughout the city. Not all were living in Paradise, and he had to make sure no one was left behind. He also had to make certain that marines stationed at the various American businesses in the city had, in fact, arrived at their posts. If they hadn't, he would have to inform Captain Brice.

Jonathan Lattimore's heart sank. He believed an evacuation was imminent, as he had been told days ago, but he had hoped he could safely keep his family in Smyrna a little while longer. He had to postpone his search for Celia's family on the Quay. At least until he could come back from Paradise with Lilian and the boys.

"As for the bread," continued Herman, "I will have it distributed within the hour. Thank you for picking it up, Jonathan. One of the other bakers and his wife dropped whatever they had left at the YMCA, as well. They were almost trampled by a mob that took a couple of loaves but, thankfully, there were people who helped them get the rest of it inside." He picked up some of the bags of bread and continued speaking.

"We'll continue to do what we can. But I don't know how much longer we can keep this going, Jonathan. This was one of the largest bakeries in the city. Captain Brice, against his orders, has placed guards at the bakery near us so, hopefully, we can rely on that one. I don't know if you will find any others open tomorrow. But ... we can hope, can't we?"

"Yes, Mr. Herman, we can. God will guide us through this. He will not forsake all these people," said Lattimore.

"He better not, sir. I don't know where they are supposed to go if He does."

Chapter 21

Smyrna's Quay

Mr. Lattimore was gracious enough to offer a stumbling and flustered Celia a hand to help her out of the car. The young girl was only too happy to accept. Jonathan did not press for further explanation. Besides, he was too busy thinking about getting his family to the theatre, as Herman had ordered.

"Celia, please, let's go to the safehouse so I can give Mrs. Kontos news of her passage," said Lattimore. Mr. Herman gave me the required paperwork for her and the children. I hope that by tonight, she can be out of the city. We can also get some water. I would like to check up on everyone there, as well, before I go see about my family in Paradise."

"Yes, Mr. Lattimore," said the young girl whose embarrassment had subsided. But she knew the search for her family had just been put off, yet again. *If Mr. Lattimore was going to Paradise for his family, he will not be escorting me any time soon,* she thought. She knew the little man would never throw her into the crowd to fend for herself, but she really wanted to find her mother and sisters. From her perspective, the sooner she was with them the better she would feel. Celia also wouldn't be a burden to the safehouse if she were with her family and she understood she had to be patient and allow Mr. Lattimore to help his. He had already done so much for the refugees.

The French consulate was in sight now, and Celia's family might be there, waiting for her. She might not need to go to the safehouse at all, she realized. As they neared the building, she saw sparse groups of people in front of it. Surely, if her mother was there, she would be visible, waiting for her in front where Celia couldn't miss her. But, again, she saw no familiar faces. She wondered if her mother and sisters had even arrived at the Quay. Passing the consulate's last waving French flag, Celia deflated. Mr. Lattimore didn't even realize what the building even meant to her. He was too consumed in his own thoughts.

The American Theatre was next to the French consulate. Celia remembered her friend, Julia, saying she wanted to see Giuseppe Verdi's *Rigoletto*—it had been playing the previous week. She wondered where Julia might be now and whether she ever got to see the opera. As she and Jonathan walked closer to the theatre, she could read the marquis. *El Dorado*, a French movie, was the attraction of the week. The theatre's doors were closed, and Celia wondered when it would reopen.

She suddenly became agitated and frustrated by the heat and she felt relieved that Mr. Lattimore was not a fast walker. Her emotions were changing constantly. She didn't even apologize when she bumped into a middle-aged woman who had her wrist wrapped in a white piece of fabric. Celia barely noticed her, and continued to walk to the safehouse, lost in her own mind. *The heat is torturing, I could walk into the ocean and not stop*, she told herself, becoming increasingly anxious.

Had there not been a mob of people on the Quay, there would be a welcome breeze coming from the harbour which would allow people to enjoy the last bits of summer freedom. The shops and restaurants would be open, and all the awnings would be lowered to keep the sun away from patrons who were still enjoying the city's waterfront. Soon, the Quay would start to become less congested in the afternoons, school would be in full swing, the tourists would be gone, and autumn would be settling into the city. How she wished for that now!

As she looked into the harbour, a flag caught Celia's eye. It was white with red rays coming from a red circle in the middle, like a rising sun. Celia had seen this flag before, but couldn't remember what country it belonged to. She couldn't make out what the men were dumping into the water, but she could see large crates continuously splashing in the harbour. Later she would learn it was a Japanese freighter whose captain had heard of the cataclysm taking place in the city. Anticipating an imminent rescue of refugees, he had ordered the dumping of thousands of dollars' worth of China, silks, and laces that were to be dropped off only a few hundred yards away at the Customs House Pier.

The growing crowd seemed to become more agitated just within the few minutes since Celia and Mr. Lattimore had dropped off the bread at the consulate. It also seemed to be denser. *How is it possible to fit more people here?* Celia wondered. When she looked into the crowd, she could no longer see any children, unless an adult were holding them in their arms. There was little space between bodies and a child would most likely have difficulty breathing if it were anywhere amongst the mass of people. The noise from the crowd had now become deafening, and the smoke coming from the southeastern part of the city was increasing. It was almost choking, at times.

It was difficult to walk without losing Mr. Lattimore and Celia hoped her teacher would be able to see her walking along the Quay again. But no one grabbed her arm this time and her thoughts ran away with her. *Where can they all be? If they were somewhere in this area, they surely would have seen me one of the three times I've passed this spot. Kyria Antigone saw me. They must not be here. They must be further south. But if they are, they're that much closer to the smoke and approaching fire.*

A part of Celia was starting to resent the refugees. Their mere presence meant she could not find her family. *Their scowls, their dirty animals, their dirty clothes, their chapped and bleeding lips. Why didn't they stay in their villages? Maybe they did something to the soldiers' families, and they deserved to be driven out of their homes? But we didn't do anything. We don't deserve to be thrown out of our city.* How she regretted having left her family! They would have been together, had she not offered to go with Voula and Kyria Eleni. If it weren't for Celia, however, they might never have run into the nurses.

As quickly as she worked herself into a cyclone, the young woman began talking herself out of it, too. She was comforted by the thought that Voula would, by now, be in a hospital, under a doctor's care, and maybe she had even given birth. Still, she missed her mother and sisters! *They must be further south, closer to where our street connects to the pier,* she thought. *That's the street they would come from, onto the Quay. If I see Kyria Antigone, I will stay with her and her sister.* Her mind raced and her eyes did, too. But she saw no one familiar in the crowd. No friends, no neighbours, no cousins, or aunts.

As she looked into the harbour, Celia bumped into an old man, who was smoking alongside two of his friends. She excused herself and walked through their cloud of smoke. The young woman became light-headed and the chaos on the street was becoming part of her mind, just as it had done when she was with Kyria Eleni and Voula. The heavy breathing, the heat, the heart palpitations. She caught herself again, making sure not to panic. She was going to be in the safehouse, soon, she remembered. It would be better inside.

People had become numb to the explosions coming from the city's inner streets to the south. Occasionally, they would be jolted by a gunshot in their vicinity, and a temporary panic would grip the mob, raising the deafening noise to the point of pain ear pain. Celia heard the shots and wondered where they were coming from. Was the victim a man who was running away, or being robbed? Or was it a woman who was no longer of any use to the soldier who had just violated her? It may even be someone fighting back, she hoped.

But Celia had come to accept that even if the last possibility were true, even if there was a push back against the soldiers, leaving the city was still the safest and most probable outcome for her and what remained of her family.

There were moments when the crowd was almost silent, and in those few seconds, everyone looked up, as if they were about to receive a signal, telling them where they could go to find food and water, or how to leave the Quay. But those moments were rare, and tension never entirely left the air. In fact, it only accentuated the ominous sensation in people's bones. Celia looked over her shoulder and saw the smoke coming from the southeast. It covered the entire Central Market, just south of the Inner Harbour and met the breeze off the harbour, in the west, creating a maelstrom upon contact. The refugees lay in its path.

Chapter 22

The Mirage Is Temporary

In Asia Minor, the month of September brings the last of the etesian winds. The term refers to the dry north winds that are familiar to the Aegean, the Ionian, and the Adriatic Seas. They appear suddenly, catching many people off guard, and sometimes force smaller yachts and ferries to remain docked. But for the experienced mariner, they're welcomed for providing a steady, leisurely wind.

Strongest in the afternoon, by nighttime the winds die down. They begin in mid-May and end in mid-September. This natural occurrence is well-known to people of the region, and beyond. The summer monsoon season of India is said to be correlated with the etesian winds and were even mentioned in ancient times.

Just weeks before the city of Smyrna was thrown into chaos, its citizens were feeling the approaching end of the yearly phenomenon. But as it was now late afternoon, the refugees were not feeling its relief and could not be bothered to ponder if the familiar winds were done for the season. They only noticed that it seemed to be getting hotter by the hour.

"Mr. Lattimore?" asked Celia, as they walked back to the safehouse. The silence between them was awkward and she wanted to do what she could to keep her mind from going to places in her head that only made her more anxious. Her parents had always taught their children that there were matters of discussion in which only adults should participate. It may not have been appropriate to ask Mr. Lattimore about the men who were terrorizing the citizens, but she had no choice. Her propensity to remain quiet was diminishing and she needed to know what to expect.

"Yes, Celia," replied the man, who was also relieved to break the silence.

"Who is Mustafa Kemal? I think he's the leader of the soldiers," said the young woman. Celia had heard the name many times, but it had always been from family members and other Greek friends. This time, she wanted to hear someone else tell her about the man who was waging war against the city.

"Yes, he is. His army came to Smyrna last week. He, himself, came into the city four days ago with his forces, but he has been pushing the Greek troops to the west, here, for weeks," said Lattimore.

"Why does he want the city so badly? And why does he want so many people to leave it? We've lived here so long. Greeks have always lived here. I remember the stories from when I was a little girl. This has always been Greek land."

Jonathan was saddened by the anguish in Celia's voice. An attempt to answer her questions was to open a discussion which would accomplish nothing now, he realized. Thankfully, Celia wasn't finished questioning. He let her continue.

"And Byzantium was a Christian city for so many years before the Turks invaded. Why now? Is it because the Greek soldiers came a few years ago? Did they do this to Turkish people when they returned?"

While Jonathan avoided discussing the past, he certainly could condemn the lack of humanity that presently had besieged the city.

"No one has done this to other people, Celia. Not that I know of, and I hope I never see this again." Celia heard Mr. Lattimore's voice quiver and noticed him shaking his head in dismay.

"Greeks have not *always* controlled this land, though."

"They were here before the Ottoman people, and they have controlled the land for a longer period of time, yes. But Kemal and other Turkish people feel this is their land now and should always be. They have their childhood stories, too, I'm sure," replied Mr. Lattimore, realizing he was doing exactly what he was trying to avoid and might be crossing into a political discussion with the young woman. As much as he wanted to help the refugees, and considered the lands to belong to Christians, the man knew enough to tread carefully when speaking with young adults or children. Something told Jonathan that the young woman was raised in a more enlightened environment, however. He took the chance to give Celia an entirely different perspective.

"He was born in Salonika, you know. Mustafa Kemal, I mean. Salonika is a city that has never been Turkish, except for the 400 years when it was under Ottoman rule. It is now Greek again, Christian. Like you, however, he wants his birthplace to remain as he remembers it was. People always want that. Look at you, now. You do not want someone else to take your home, your land. The Trojans didn't want the Greeks taking their city, either. Did you know that Neoptolemus, Achilles' son, threw Hektor's infant son over the walls of the city?"

"Yes, so that the boy wouldn't grow up to seek revenge on the Greek and his family," replied Celia.

"That's correct. But imagine being a Trojan. How would you feel if someone did that to a child today?" asked Jonathan. He could see the girl lower her eyes. She looked back at the American and nodded. Kyria Eleni had said something similar earlier that day. The myths and legends Celia had always heard and been proud of were becoming flawed.

"Youth is most precious to people, whether it's their own childhood that they remember from their past, or the youthfulness today that belongs to their precious children. But God will help us all. Jesus did not want to strike down his enemies, remember. He had patience and accepted everyone into His ways just by speaking to them." Jonathan smiled as he spoke with conviction and optimism. Celia listened and, for a few moments, forgot the faces on the Quay.

"In America, my dear, we have taught the natives about Jesus. The Indian people there have embraced Him. And we, as Christians must continue to show them the way to God and Jesus. We have opened schools for their children, taught them how to speak and serve God." Lattimore's chest seemed to puff up as he spoke. His demeanour changed, though, as he looked around.

"But here, we have a little more work to do. More history to consider. We just need to find a way to be humane to one another. To be kind to one another as God wants us to be." Lattimore finished his sentence with a hint of anger in his voice, something the young girl hadn't noticed until now.

The day's experiences had questioned humanity's capacity for malevolence. But it had not questioned Jonathan's faith in God. He firmly believed he was in Smyrna to help as many of His children as possible and remind them that He was still with them on the Quay. Even Mr. Lattimore could see that many of His flock were losing faith, however. And he recognized that the young girl next to him could soon become one of them.

Celia glanced toward the ocean and another cormorant caught her attention. With the seabird in mind, she began to imagine herself as another; a pelican, trying to stretch her neck as much as she could, looking for friends, relatives, neighbours, other teachers. No one was there. No one she could identify, at least. It was hard to believe that with so many people in sight, not one was familiar. The familiar is what would keep Celia connected to her past, and all that she knew. She was determined to hold on to that. She couldn't move forward without it ... alone. And as she moved further north towards the safehouse, she knew the chances of seeing someone familiar would diminish. They were people from the countryside, beaten, separated from loved ones, robbed. But none were familiar.

As she and Mr. Lattimore approached the mansion, she looked up at the American flag flapping outside the second-floor balcony. She hadn't noticed it earlier but understood that the flag could be the reason the building had not been attacked by the soldiers. She hadn't seen any of them roaming the Quay, but she began to wonder if soldiers would break into the safehouse, especially since the mansion had so many beautiful items left behind from the previous owner. *Soldiers are animals. They're capable of anything!*

Before entering the building, she noticed there were many smaller fishing boats moored close to the safehouse, some with refugees in them. But even Celia knew that the trek across the Aegean wouldn't get them far.

Lattimore opened the door for her. The smell of death and birth hit her simultaneously, as she walked inside. It was only logical as both involved blood, sweat, and tears, but she had become too tired to care what the smell was like. *I don't want to be here any longer. Not in this oven, and especially not wearing this jacket!* She quickly realized how miserable she had become and almost infantile in her attitude. *If no one in this building were to speak to me again, I'd be quite content.*

"Mr. Lattimore!" someone called, from another part of the building; someone who somehow already knew the man had entered the building.

"Yes, I am coming," he replied and proceeded to walk to the back area of the home.

Tired, Celia stood over the mosaic in the front hallway and stared at it. What was happening in the building was an extension of what was going on outside, and yet it was a totally different world. The stench and heat were worse, but the people inside were not threatening. On the Quay, even the gentlest people had now become vicious. In the mansion, kindness and patience gave its occupants some hope. They didn't fight one another for a mat, or food, or attention. It was peaceful, even with the children crying or the women's injuries and labour pains. It was the closest thing to heaven at that moment, Celia thought to herself, leaning up against the wall.

Instantly, her head began to pound, and she leaned forward, cupping her ears. The pulse of her heart echoed through the blood rushing in her temples and the back of her eyes. Her heart raced, her limbs were weighing heavy, and her head stopped pounding but began to spin. She couldn't understand what was happening to her. Was it the lack of food or water, the heat, or the embarrassing moment at the American consulate? Was it the overwhelming uncertainty of the future? She could not begin to answer any of the questions that had been accumulating in her head all morning. The fear of not having any answers to her questions, and not being able to see a familiar face, had brought her to a standstill. *I just want to go home,* she told herself and started taking deep breaths. She did not want to fall apart and start crying. It wouldn't change her situation.

Leaning her back up against the nearest wall again she closed her eyes, but that made it worse. The room was spinning faster now and, instinctively, she raised one arm outward to find balance. Startled that she had hit someone, she immediately opened her eyes. It was Maisie, the nurse who had taken Voula to the hospital. For a second time in the last hour, Celia could feel her face turning red and erupt with overwhelming emotion. The young girl fell onto the nurse's shoulders and began to sob. Maisie wasn't someone she had known for years, but she was still familiar. And Celia was delighted to see her.

The nurse, who was not totally surprised by the young woman's tearful outburst, comforted her for a few moments and then gently held her by the arms. After Celia settled down and wiped her eyes, Maisie let go of her.

"Celia, correct?" asked the nurse.

"Yes, that is my name. How is Voula?" inquired the teenager, stopping her tears almost immediately. The only sign left of her anguish were her red eyes.

"She is well," smiled the nurse. "She gave birth minutes after arriving at the hospital. She had a healthy baby boy. They both need to rest as much as they can for the journey," said Maisie. "Kyria Eleni had gone to the French consulate to see about passage, but I don't know if she was successful. I imagine she was."

"Oh, a boy! That is very good news." Celia exclaimed, with a sudden change of emotion. While her joy was genuine, even she couldn't distinguish if her remaining tears were the remnants of despair or due to the good news about Voula.

"Yes, it is wonderful. They were both very lucky to have had your help. Are you staying here at the safehouse with us?" asked Maisie.

"I don't really know. I am supposed to find my mother and sisters on the Quay, with Mr. Lattimore's help," Celia replied, still sniffling and trying to dry her eyes. "But I overheard Mr. Herman tell Mr. Lattimore that all Americans need to be evacuated." Celia hoped that mentioning her own predicament would trigger an offer of help from the young nurse, but Maisie didn't bite.

"Oh, I see," she said instead with a look of concern. Before she could continue, Celia saw Jane descending the staircase.

"Celia, you're back," said the older nurse.

"Yes, Mr. Lattimore and I returned a few minutes ago. Can I go look for my family now?" she asked. "I know Mr. Lattimore may not be able to take me, but I'll go alone, if I have to." Celia was willing to do anything to see her sisters and mother. But Jane did not have her usual confident and self-assured look on her face. She looked apprehensive about what she was about to say.

"I was going to ask if you could come with Maisie and me back toward the Dutch hospital, to an Armenian orphanage. They are not far from the hospital, and the situation is quite serious. The two women there are trying to evacuate the children from the building and take them to the YWCA. Fires are breaking out throughout the city, and that building is in its path. They can't do it alone as there are more than a hundred children to be moved. You said you speak some Armenian, yes?" Jane sounded concerned, but calm.

"We need to keep as many doctors and nurses as possible with the sick, but your extra pair of hands and eyes would help us terribly. We need to bring those children back here to the Quay. Or at least get them out of harm's way."

Celia was too embarrassed to refuse the woman. It was evident that the nurses were both exhausted, and neither spoke Greek or Armenian. They had found someone who was not capable of helping with the sick or pregnant but could be used to do other work. Celia was young, willing, and, as they soon realized, capable of overcoming the scenes of brutality better than most young women. The teenager was tall and swift. And as shy and introverted as she seemed at times, her presence emanated a sense of composure and competence. She listened and obeyed, and her compassion towards Voula told them they could appeal to her for help. It was possible that they believed the young girl's hope of being reunited with her family was idealistic, and an exercise in futility. Her time would be better spent helping than looking for her people, who might already be dead. Jane's request fell on the right person. Celia agreed to help.

"My Armenian is not very good, but I can help," she offered almost without emotion; she felt defeated. But she saw no way to refuse.

"Wonderful," replied Jane, who was already putting on her large hat. "Thank you, Celia. Those children and those teachers will be very grateful." And the nurse meant it. Her smile and one-arm hug over the young girl's shoulder showed it. But Celia wanted to get the job done as quickly as possible so she could get back to the Quay and begin looking for her family. *If Mr. Lattimore goes to Paradise for his family and I go help with the orphans, maybe we'll be back here at the same time, and he can take me to the southern part of the Quay.* She kept hoping that by the end of the day, she would be with her mother.

Within minutes the three women were back onto the streets. They had to push through the mob of people that continued to grow by the hour. For that reason, they decided to turn down the first side street to avoid losing each other in the crowd. The nurses walked quickly, but Celia was more than capable of keeping up with them.

Bodies and broken doors were evidence that the soldiers were moving closer to the Quay. But much of the damage was also caused by irregulars, who preyed on the refugees, too. When Celia slowed to take a closer look at the destruction, she would catch herself and look just enough to realize she shouldn't have. Her fear was always that she would know the person lying in the dirt. For the time being, she was fortunate.

Celia also told herself it would be cruel of God to have her recognize a dead body in the streets and not one living soul on the Quay. *Or did He intend for Kyria Antigone to be my only gift? A momentary gift I had to give away.* By the next block, she decided to make sure she was keeping pace with Jane and Maisie and try to ignore the bodies.

As they walked, the three women wondered if these were people who had been in hiding over the last few days and that the fires had now forced them to the streets. These people were carrying fewer household items, probably having decided to leave most of their belongings behind or perhaps they had lost them to a fire or a thief; they smelled of smoke and sweat.

The orphanage was southeast of the Dutch hospital, just north of the Jewish quarter, where there were no reports of fires. But a fire had begun further west in the Armenian sector, and it was spreading.

The people they passed on the street—who came from the rural areas, east of the city—were walking towards the Quay wearing the same wretched faces of desperation, hunger, and thirst. But they had not seen the situation on the Quay, yet.

The countryside had seen much more unrest in recent years. It wasn't like Smyrna. There was no tolerance or diversity in the rural parts of Ionia. The newest soldiers to enter a village would justify their actions by reminding their victims of unsettled debts. Some who were walking into the city had endured enough from all sides and abandoned their homes, deciding it was best to head for Smyrna's tolerant society. Their shoes and clothing were dustier than those fleeing the Greek or Armenian Quarters. Their faces were more parched and burned by the sun. But none had the soot of the fires on them. A few of them, recognizing that Maisie and Jane were nurses, would stop and ask for help. All the nurses could do was direct them to a safehouse, or the Quay, if they looked healthy enough.

"Is there more than one safehouse on the Quay?" asked Celia.

"Not on the Quay, but there's a second just around the corner from the Sporting Club. And Mr. Lattimore was able to secure a third on Frank Street," replied Jane. "For now, they are only providing shelter, because there are very few beds or supplies. But even that is a blessing for some people."

Celia only nodded and looked down at the cobblestone road.

As they came upon an intersection, a car crossed their path. It had an Italian flag attached to its mirror and inside the vehicle there were seven or eight people piled up, heading for the Quay. Celia watched them slowly approach the waterfront, and three soldiers appeared from a building, pointing their rifles at them, ordering them to stop. Had it not been for Maisie, gently pushing her, Celia would have frozen in her tracks watching the scene unfold less than fifty feet away from her. All three soldiers wore fezzes, but one had a moustache and a cigarette hanging from his mouth. Celia stared at the man and her breathing intensified, but she continued to walk.

As the three women walked through the intersection, they saw the occupants give their identification papers to the soldiers. It became apparent to the teenager that the nurses had tried to inconspicuously pick up their pace. They also walked closer to Celia, in a moving huddle. She had no identification papers, and she was Greek. Thankfully, the soldiers' attention was focused on the car and not the three women.

"Maisie, have you met Mr. Lattimore's family, at all?" asked Jane, in a tone unlike her, almost as if to gossip. Celia was struck by the oddity but welcomed the distraction. "I understand Mr. Lattimore has gone to Paradise to get them. I was hoping to meet Mrs. Lattimore before she left the city," continued Jane.

"No, I haven't," Maisie replied. "It was about time orders were given to leave the city. They should have had people out sooner," said the nurse who sounded equally odd. Celia didn't comment. She didn't want to utter a word that might be overheard by someone looking for a Greek or an Armenian.

As they got closer to their destination, there were more corpses and more homes that had been broken into or vandalized. Many of the bodies lying in the street were now swollen, some of them half- or entirely naked, and some in peculiar positions. Death was indiscriminate, as the victims were young, old, male, and female. Even children had been brutally murdered. As the wind kept changing, the smell of the smoke alternated with the smell of decomposing bodies. Celia couldn't help but put her hand to her nose, for the little good it did.

By the time they arrived at the orphanage, Celia had become numb to the scenes in the streets. She stopped asking herself why people could do such things and decided that Mr. Lattimore's hope for humanity was unrealistic, almost romantic. *Even animals do not do this to each other,* she told herself, bitterly. *I can't believe I lived in the same city as these demons. But that will change, soon.* Her focus was on the new task she was asked to participate in. Even her posture was starting to shift. She stood taller and alert.

Chapter 23

Saving the Innocents

When they arrived at the front door, Celia didn't wait for the nurses to open it. She pushed it and walked in first. Maisie looked at Jane and faintly smiled, as both nurses noticed Celia's growing confidence.

Just inside the vestibule, they were met by Mary Eriksson and Hazel Moore, both American; and behind them were 150 little girls wearing blue dresses with gold-coloured aprons. Dr. Preston from the Dutch hospital was also at the orphanage, having come to help the two women evacuate the children. What Celia didn't know was that on the other side of the building, hundreds of refugees—seeking protection from the Turkish soldiers just beyond the iron gate—had locked themselves in the courtyard. The soldiers knew that sooner or later, the refugees would have to leave the orphanage, and they stood waiting for them to attempt an escape. It was more efficient to use knives and swords than to waste bullets.

Expecting help to arrive soon, the two teachers had already organized their charges into a double column.

"We're ready to go," said Miss Eriksson after Jane introduced herself and the other two women.

"Tell us how we can help," replied Maisie.

The group of adults began to move the girls out, with Miss Moore holding a pole with an American flag atop. Because this building was officially Armenian, there were no guards to help in the evacuation, as was happening in some of the other properties across the city.

Miss Moore and Miss Eriksson led the girls, Maisie and Celia were in the middle, and Dr. Preston and Jane brought up the rear. The plan was to get the children to the YWCA many blocks away, where they could be escorted to the Quay by American guards.

As Celia followed the children out the doors, she noticed the dust was greater and the heat was more intense than it had been even minutes earlier. Looking to her left, she saw the fire was fast approaching the building, and through its rear gates, she saw arms pointing towards herself and the procession.

"Miss Lane!" she called out to the nurse. Maisie looked at Celia, who pointed to her left. "The fire is not far. And there are people behind that gate!"

"Just keep walking," replied Maisie. "We'll be safe."

Celia nodded and remained calm, keeping her eyes on the children ahead, making sure they stayed in line.

About two-thirds of the group had already left the orphanage when the refugees in the courtyard noticed the girls were being evacuated. Realizing that this was their best chance to try to flee the oncoming fire and the soldiers, they flung open the gates and raced to catch up and blend into the line of little girls.

While Celia initially was angered by their opportunistic behaviour, many of them were holding children of their own, and the looks of desperation and fear made the young woman realize everyone had a right to try to survive. The abrupt exodus immediately caused a panic, and the soldiers began to attack the refugees.

"*Prosohi! Stamata!*" Celia called out to a few people, who had now pushed and knocked down some of the orphans. Yelling at them to be careful and stop was senseless. The pandemonium wouldn't allow her voice to be heard, let alone accepted. Celia also forgot that the children and the refugees were Armenian.

The screaming, gunshots and explosions from the fires were piercing, causing her to feel the vibrations in her head. She saw two people fall to the ground, not far from the line of orphans, both shot. She wanted to stop, but she didn't want to leave the children. Besides, to stop now would only make her an easy target. Celia's mind went into a tailspin, and she couldn't understand where all the people were coming from. Her hair was loosening from her ponytail as she spun her head constantly trying to see where to go, and who was coming at her. She couldn't run too fast, as the children wouldn't be able to keep up, but the refugees ran for their lives. They knocked, pushed, or stumbled on anything or anyone in their way.

"I can't do this!" Celia screamed to Maisie, as she tried to cover her ears.

"Yes, you can. You have no choice, Celia! Keep moving. NOW!" shouted the nurse, who sharply pointed to the road ahead. Her words and actions startled Celia. With a frightened look on her face the young woman obeyed, nodding to Maisie.

She looked down at the children who were told not to look back. One little girl's eyes were wide, and she was almost smiling, as if this was a race or some other sort of game. Celia was glad for that and thought to herself that if the children could continue running, she certainly could.

As she saw some of the orphans pushed or on the ground, she immediately began using her body and arms to keep anyone else from breaking through the girls' lines. It was impossible to control so many people. She looked to Maisie, who was doing the same thing, holding the hand of one little girl she had just picked up off the ground. A young man next to her saw the nurse's irritation and he too, began to hold others from overwhelming the line of children.

"*Ditek yerekhanerin!*" he called out in Armenian, being mindful of the children. Out of the corner of her eye, Maisie saw a soldier coming at the man with his bayonet. The nurse gasped only for a second, before she readied herself. She let go of the little girl's hand, grabbed the hardcover Bible she had under her other arm, and slapped it into the face of the soldier. He instantly fell to the ground.

As Celia looked at the disoriented soldier, she could hear the bells of Saint Stephanos ringing in the background. It was 4:00 and the sun had passed its peak. She looked up from the soldier and could see through the windows of the building directly next to her that the fire had caught up with the group. She began to gently push the children forward, telling them to hurry in her broken Armenian. Looking over her shoulder as she moved forward, she could see the flames were soaring beyond the building's roof.

Kemal's army was finally ridding the city of the infidels and what they had built. They had little use for the homes, stores, and churches that were crumbling to the ground and whose cinders were landing on those fleeing. The column of children had been broken, but most of them were still grouped together.

Celia was next to one of the smallest girls in the orphanage; she was so terrified, she started to turn around in circles. The little girl's blond hair was in two braids, and she held a little wooden horse in her hands. Panicked about what was happening to the child, Celia snatched her up and continued to walk quickly, trying not to lose sight of the American flag Miss Moore was carrying.

After a few minutes of chaos, and realizing she wasn't strong enough to carry the girl for too long, she put the child back on the ground and told her not to let go of her hand. If she had held her in her arms any longer, she wouldn't have been able to keep an eye on the other children in the line, or they would fall behind in the crowd, and both be lost.

Celia turned to look for Maisie, but the nurse had moved ahead, out of Celia's sight which was exactly what Celia had feared. She couldn't see Jane or the doctor, either. As she glanced back to see if there were any children left straggling, she saw that the orphanage was fully engulfed in flames. Only the wooden supports remained. It didn't take long for the fire to consume the building, and within seconds it collapsed within itself, sending cinders and grey smoke into the sky.

The smoke and chaos made it difficult for the adults to stay focused on the direction they were heading while making sure none of the children were hit with embers or other projectiles from the blazing buildings. The heat was intense; the temples of every soul were draped with sweat. Celia was tempted to remove her jacket and lose the gold coin in its hem. But in her mind, to leave it behind was like leaving a part of her family in the dirt. She told herself that she had already left enough in what would soon be ashes of her home. Her brother and father were all she was ready to abandon in Smyrna. It was out of the question to leave something her mother had made for her with something that could buy her way out of the inferno. She wouldn't remove her jacket. Not yet.

As if they understood the severity of the situation, the children remained calm and quiet, even while the screaming refugees were separating them from their teachers and the others. Celia and the little blonde girl had been pushed by the refugees and in the chaos, ended up moving in the wrong direction. Once she realized they were lost, Celia stopped. Making certain not to panic the child, the young woman held her ground, looking around to get her bearings while pushing people away to keep them from moving her and the little girl any further.

"Don't worry," she said to the little girl, sheepishly smiling, trying to keep her calm. She knew the child didn't speak Greek, but hoped her gestures would suffice. The smoke had trickled into their lungs, casting tiny little webs, only enough to be a nuisance. Both coughed simultaneously, and Celia again, smiled at the little one, who beamed back with a grin of her own, not understanding the desperation of their predicament. The innocence and trust from the child gave Celia a burst of courage and caused her to chuckle. "Yes, we will just follow the sun!" she shouted to the little one. She knew where it was this time of the day. Holding the child's hand with her right hand and using her left to shield herself from anyone coming at them, Celia figured out which way they needed to go, even if they had to go alone. Once again, the teen girl picked up the orphan and looked for the American flag. She headed towards the sun, but soon enough saw the closer marker.

"There it is!" Celia shouted to the child. She pointed it out to the little girl, who put her arms up in the air like she had just won a prize and cried out in victory.

Fortunately, the flag was not too far, and they were able to catch up to the group that had been split in different directions. Soon enough, however, the relentless American teachers and medical staff were able to push through the crowd, stop for a moment and reassemble the girls.

"Celia," called out Maisie, "I thought we had lost you. I didn't see you in the line."

"No," Celia replied, with relief. "Not lost yet." Celia looked at the little girl and smiled, as she put her down.

"Good," replied the nurse, smiling and pulling the scattered children back in line.

They continued their route, in the original two-by-two formation.

As the buildings burned and collapsed next to them, some of the evacuees noticed rats running in groups of their own down the streets. The fire had brought a new enemy to the scene. Just as Mr. Lattimore had said earlier to Celia, they too, were looking for a way out of the fire's path. The sight repulsed those who cared to look. And as scared and as frenzied, the vermin were heading in the same direction as the people … towards the pier.

Chapter 24

Who Stays Behind?

Arriving at the YWCA, the group's stay was short-lived. The one American woman in charge of that building, Miss Heather Chamberlain, was also organizing the evacuation of the women and children staying there. Luck was finally on their side, however. This was an American organization, and, therefore, guards had been placed at this building. Soon after the orphans arrived, everyone headed for the consulate, which was only one street away. Unfortunately, not all the little Armenian girls had made it to the YWCA. Some had slipped out of the column and had either become lost or trampled.

Celia and Maisie went with the group of women and children from the YWCA to the consulate, but Miss Moore continued with the orphans in their blue and gold aprons to the Quay. She knew the children would not be given passage on American ships, and so two sailors offered to escort the children and their teacher to the waterfront.

Before they parted, Celia knelt to say goodbye to the little girl she had in her care and kissed her on the forehead. The little blonde girl hugged the young woman and ran to get back in line, following Miss Moore. *One woman with over one hundred little girls.* Celia watched them leave and silently prayed they would get safely to the Quay. It deeply bothered her that some children were allowed to stay with the consulate, while others, including Celia's little blonde girl, had to wait on the Quay with everyone else. She would have gone with them, but she didn't want Maisie to walk back to the safehouse alone and she also didn't want to remain responsible for the girls once they all arrived at the Quay. At least at the safehouse, she could purposefully begin to look for her family, she supposed.

Celia and Maisie waved to the girls, smiling and watching until the last one turned the corner. As they began walking down the streets again, they both realized how thirsty and hungry they were.

"There's some bread left at the safehouse. We'll be there soon," said the nurse, who saw Celia put her hand to her stomach.

"I'm fine, Miss Lane. Thank you. I'm not very hungry. I had some fresh bread with Mr. Lattimore earlier today. The faces of some people coming into the city ... you can tell they haven't eaten recently." She tried to appear strong and resilient. She would do anything to eat her mother's lamb kebab or lentil rice ... or even the grapes Maria had put in their bag.

She looked around her to see if there were any fig, plum, or peach trees in the vicinity. It was normal for passersby to pluck a ripened treat from a branch hanging over a fence onto the street. At this time of year, some of those trees may still have the last of their fruit. But only one fig tree could be seen, and as she walked closer to it, she saw the tree had nothing to offer. As disappointing as it was to see, Celia hoped that it was refugees who had stripped the tree of its fruit, and not soldiers. And for now, food and water could wait. Survival from fire and soldiers were of greater concern.

On their route, Maisie continued to tell the young girl about her job. She was from a small town in New Brunswick, Canada. She had seen similar atrocities committed on the coast of the Black Sea against ethnic Greeks prior to coming to Smyrna and had taken care of sick and wounded orphans in Marsovan and Samsun. She was in her late thirties, but her energy was that of a twenty-five-year-old warrior.

Celia was humbled by what Maisie described. She knew that both the nurses she met that day were single and had devoted their lives to helping people they did not know. In Celia's world, women married and had children. She was hoping to become a teacher, but still wanted to marry and have a family one day. The only nurses she knew went home every day to their husbands and children. They did not travel to the other side of the world to take care of orphans or anyone else.

As they rounded the corner onto the Quay, Celia noticed an American destroyer was particularly close to the pier. It had been anchored at Passport Pier, where an intense smoke had blown north from the Central Market. The *USS Litchfield* was just over 300 feet long and weighed more than 1200 tons. While it would remain in the harbour, it was sailing away from the pier to drop anchor, having just evacuated many Americans.

Captain Brice had boarded the ship after inspecting the city. While the *Litchfield* was tied up at the Quay, it was a fast ship and a quick slip could be made, if needed. What he had seen and heard throughout the day, made Brice very nervous. He had an ominous feeling that the worst was yet to come and knew he had to prepare for it. He was also not impressed with many of the crew who had allowed many of the American nationals in Paradise to bring their Greek and Armenian servants aboard the ship.

But as Celia looked at the colossal steel refuge slowly leaving the pier, she couldn't help but be envious of those on board. *How lucky they are to be off the Quay* she thought. She hoped her mother and sisters were aboard and could somehow find a way to rescue her. *Mama could use the coins she has with her.*

Approaching the American theatre, the two women were stopped by a group of American guards who had formed a human passageway. Sailors in two lines created a path of a few feet wide, shielding the remaining American nationals as they passed through and headed to the whaleboats that were waiting for them. These whaleboats would take their passengers, ten at a time, to the *USS Simpson*. One sailor would stand at the seawall and when the boat was in place, he would signal to the theatre, and his shipmate would allow the next ten people to head for the pier.

Onlooking refugees attempted to break through the lines, pleading to be taken on board. But the sailors managed to hold their line, at times forced to beat women away from their only plausible escape. Some of them were offering their children to the people boarding the whaleboats, but no one would take them. The noise was so deafening Maisie had to put one hand to her ear, and raised her shoulder to the other, as she still held onto her Bible.

"Excuse me, sir, we need to get to the other side," she called to one soldier, who ignored her. She repeated her request. "Please, sir, we need to get to the other side. We are helping with the relief effort and need to get to the other side. We're not trying to board the whaleboats!"

As she yelled out to the man, she pointed to the other side of the street, and not towards the open sea. The sailor nodded. He came closer to Maisie so she could hear him.

"Once the doors to the theatre close, and those people pass, we will disperse. In just a few minutes, you will be able to cross to the other side!" he called out. Maisie nodded her understanding of his direction and looked back at the theatre. She saw the door close and once the remaining Americans passed her, she pulled Celia by the hand, pushing through the crowd that was still hoping to sneak through to salvation.

As they walked past the line, Celia noticed Mrs. Kontos and her children were the last in the procession of people. She was being helped by another woman who was holding the hand of the little girl. The boys each carried a small suitcase, while the young mother carried another. *She did it*, thought the young girl. *If we could all be so fortunate,.*

Looking out into the harbour, she was able to see there were now more boats coming to and leaving the pier, and unlike what Celia had seen earlier, they carried more than just five or six people. They were transporting people to the larger ships, some that were anchored further away than the *Litchfield. Finally,* Celia thought, as she inhaled for a sigh of relief, stench and all. Celia had become indifferent to the smell. She had become a warrior in the eyes of children and adults alike. But the idea of glory was nowhere in Celia's mind … her only thought was to return to her family, her home, her dreams. For now, however, Mr. Lattimore's haven was all that she could be grateful for, as she pushed her way through the mob, holding fast to Maisie's hand.

The two continued towards the safehouse at 490 on the Quay in the formerly affluent area of Bella Vista, which now reeked of destitution and misery. Greek and Armenian refugees were stuck on the Quay, surrounded by the fire and hounded by an enemy who was closing in on them. Their only immediate escape was either to the heavens above them or the ships in the harbour. Like an extending open palm of God, the whaleboats had become Sanctuary.

Chapter 25

The Same But Different

Vicki sat sideways in the living room armchair and when she finished her grandmother's journal, she let the little book rest on her chest. Squinting as she tried to remember, she thought about the last time she had been in Greece, in 1978, a year before Celia had died.

Yiayia and I lay in her squeaky brass bed for the afternoon siesta. It was so horribly hot. I don't remember how the topic of Smyrna came up, but I do remember she told me about a young woman who was beautiful and that soldiers took her into a room. She said being beautiful was sometimes a curse. And later, when they brought the young woman out, they tied her to two horses and made the animals run in opposite directions. Vicki's eyes suddenly became globes, and her lips softly separated. The story had stuck in her head for years. *Oh my God! I thought Yiayia was confused…that she was skipping parts of the story, or making it up. I think it happened! That horrible incident she described must have actually happened!*

She missed her grandmother terribly and didn't know why. They hadn't spent much time together and except for that one little bit of information she had given to her that summer day, Vicki got very few words from the woman. But her name, alone, connected them. She wished she were still alive and coming to her wedding. Knowing the few little snippets of her teenage life brought Celia closer to her granddaughter, brought her to life. And the fact she had wanted to be a teacher brought her especially closer to Vicki's life.

I wouldn't even care if she came to the wedding. I just want to ask her so many questions. Did they leave Smyrna the next day? Next week? What stopped her from becoming a teacher when they got to Greece?

Vicki sighed and got up to return the notebook to the drawer. Suddenly, she felt a huge wave of compassion for her grandmother and everyone else who had endured the misery of genocide. Vicki realized she had been lucky, growing up in a country that was far removed from the bloodshed of war. And she had a new respect for the mysteries of her grandmother's stoicism. She had survived, obviously. But at what cost?

Vicki tucked the little book in to its resting place and closed the drawer. She could never forget the tale of what her Yiayia had endured. And she would never stop wondering what else had happened in that dear lady's life. It was mysterious and touching. As with all compelling stories, Vicki wanted to know more.

Unbeknownst to her and the rest of the world, there was much more to Celia's story…

Bibliography:

- Sakayan, Dora. "An Armenian Doctor in Turkey. Garabed Hatcherian: My Smyrna Ordeal of 1922", 1997

- Hirschon, Renee. "Heirs of the Greek Catastrophe. The Social Life of Asia Minor Refugees in Piraeus", Berghahn Books. New York. 1989

- Milton, Giles. "Paradise Lost. Smyrna 1922: The Destruction of Islam's City of Tolerance", John Murray. London. 2008

- Lovejoy Pohl, Esther. "Certain Samaritans", MacMillan, N.Y. 1933

- Ureneck, Lou. "The Great Fire. One American's Mission to Rescue - Victims of the 20th Century's First Genocide. Harper Collins, N.Y. 2015

Manor House Publishing Inc.
wwww.manor-house-publishing.com
905-648-4797